OFFICE MATE

MILFORD COLLEGE

NOELLE ADAMS

This book is a work of fiction. Names, characters, places, and incidents are the product of the author's imagination or are used fictitiously. Any resemblance to actual events, locales, or persons, living or dead, is coincidental.

Copyright © 2019 by Noelle Adams. All rights reserved, including the right to reproduce, distribute, or transmit in any form or by any means.

1

THERE SHOULD BE A RULE AGAINST COLLEGES DROPPING unwanted English professors into the offices of nice, unsuspecting members of the history faculty.

There is no rule, of course. Colleges can assign office space as they like. Which is why I'm being forced to share my beautiful office with the new guy in the English department. The beginning of a new school year in the fall is usually my favorite time of year, but I'm not looking forward to this semester.

At all.

Space is always at a premium on college campuses—particularly small schools like Milford College, which doesn't have a big endowment or a lot of rich donors. I understand having to juggle and rejuggle available space, and I'm usually a good-natured and flexible employee. But full-time faculty here have always gotten their own office, and it's hard not to be annoyed by the fact that I'm suddenly forced to double up with someone new.

I lucked out two years ago when I was first hired at Milford, a small liberal arts college in the middle of nowhere in south central Virginia. A long-standing member of the history department had just retired, and I ended up with his office on the fourth floor of the main academics building. It's a big, quirky space with strange angles, a slanted ceiling, and two big windows. I've fixed it up with pretty wall hangings, curtains, throw rugs, and knickknacks. The office is exactly the way I want it, and I love coming in to work every morning and seeing it.

But evidently the office is too big. It's always had two desks, and I should have been more strategic and asked the folks in facilities to move the second desk out of the office when I first arrived so it wouldn't be such a tempting target. But the second desk was convenient. I used it for students taking makeup tests or if I needed a clear workspace to grade papers or spread out notes for a research project.

And now my office is going to be invaded by a new assistant professor—one I don't know and who isn't even in my department.

I'm trying not to be sulky or resentful, but it's a struggle.

It's my office. I'm thirty years old and have a PhD in early American history. I don't have a very impressive salary because the college is small and my discipline is not in high demand. I teach four classes a semester and one in the January interim term. I'm the advisor to the history club, and I sit on three different faculty committees. The least they can give me is my own office.

I'm grumbling about it at lunch on a Friday in late August to my best friend, Jennifer.

"Marcus said they did try to find some other way to get you both your own office," Jennifer says with a sympathetic look. She works in the financial aid department, and her fiancé is the director of facilities at Milford. "But they just couldn't work it out."

"I know." I took the biggest piece of coconut pie to try to assuage my wounded psyche, and I take a bite of it now, the sweet softness soothing on my tongue. "I'm sure they did everything they could. It's not Marcus's fault."

"He feels bad about it. We know you love your office. But it will just be a year, and maybe it will be kind of fun."

"Yeah. Maybe." The thought perks me up a little. "I did have fun with my office mate in graduate school. She ended up being one of my best friends. I think I'd feel better if I'd actually met the guy. I was visiting Mom and Dad when he came for his campus interview. But everyone was really impressed with him. Hopefully he'll be nice and friendly. You met him, didn't you?"

Jennifer is pretty with shoulder-length, light brown hair and intelligent brown eyes. Unlike me, she has a way of coming across as serious and in control. I, on the other hand, have blue eyes that are too big, a baby face with too many curves and dimples, and a round figure that looks all wrong in tailored, professional clothes. I was made for long, soft skirts and pretty tunic tops, and my long, dark hair is always slipping out of any braid or bun I try to contain it in. I used to try to wear suits and look dignified, but I gave that up a long time ago.

"Yes, I met him," Jennifer says after a noticeable pause. "He seems incredibly smart."

"Smart? *Smart*?" My eyes get even bigger than they normally are. "That's all you can say about him?"

"Well, I didn't get to know him. I just said hello and listened to his research talk." She frowns, and I see something quite clear in that expression. "He seems very serious, but very... polite."

"Polite!" I say it too loudly. The students eating lunch around us turn and look. I lower my voice. "Polite? Oh God, you didn't like him, did you?"

"I didn't *not* like him. I just didn't get a good sense of him. I'm sure it will be fine." She's obviously trying to be encouraging, but it's not working on me.

Jennifer is naturally reserved. Not nearly as expressive as I am. But I can read the hesitation in her expression.

"It's not going to be fine," I groan with exaggerated despair. "It's going to be terrible."

"What's going to be terrible?" Marcus Greene sits down beside Jennifer with his lunch tray. He's a handsome man with striking blue-gray eyes and an easy grin. He's giving it to me now. "Whatever it is can't be that bad."

"It is bad. I have to share my office with an asshole."

"He's not an asshole," Jennifer objects with a little laugh. "I didn't say anything of the kind."

"Who, Jones? I don't think he's an asshole." Marcus pulls his eyebrows together. "Just kind of... serious."

I groan again. "It's going to be terrible."

Jennifer laughs again, and Marcus drapes a casual arm around the back of her chair. His eyes on her face are soft and fond, and I feel the briefest flicker of jealousy.

No man has ever looked at me that way. I know it for sure.

I brush the feeling aside because it's unworthy. I get plenty of male interest, and that's not what gives me value anyway.

"We did try to free up an office for him," Marcus says. "I came up with several different configurations, but none of them worked."

"I thought you said he could take Cole's office. He's hardly ever there anyway."

"That was our first choice since Cole is in the English department and retiring next year. But he wouldn't give it up."

I snarl. "He's seriously only in his office a few hours a week."

"I know. But he's a full professor, and he's not retired yet. We couldn't force him out of the office." Marcus looks resigned. He's obviously fought many of these battles with faculty before. "And the only other available space was in the science building. The English folks were not okay with having their new guy all the way across campus. So sharing it is. Just for a year."

"Yeah. Just for a year." I try again to fight the reluctance. "I'm sure it will be just fine. I'm a nice person, right?"

"Right," Marcus and Jennifer say at the same time.

"People usually like me."

"Everyone loves you," Jennifer says. "Everyone I ever talk to tells me how amazing you are. Sweet and funny and good at getting to know people. I'm sure Dr. Jones will love you too."

I've finished my coconut pie and now lean back in my chair. "But why does he have to be a Milton scholar?"

Marcus and Jennifer exchange looks. "What's wrong with Milton?" Jennifer asks. "Isn't he a good writer?"

"Of course he's a good writer! But imagine being able to choose anyone in all of literature to focus on and choosing John Milton. Who *does* that? What does that say about this guy? And all anyone will tell me about him is that he's smart and serious."

"And polite," Marcus says with a twitch of his lips. "I thought he was very polite."

I groan again and sink my head onto my hands. "I've got to spend a whole year sharing my beautiful office with a smart, serious, polite John Milton scholar! Can you think of anything worse?"

Jennifer and Marcus laugh, as I knew they would. I'm playing up my distress on purpose.

But still...

I'm not entirely making it up.

I have some very real concerns about this man I'm being forced to share my office with.

He doesn't sound like a friendly, flexible kind of person. I hope I can manage to win him over.

I GO BACK to my office after lunch to finish putting my syllabus together for one of my fall classes. Actual classes don't start until a week from Monday, but the administration wants all the major course documents prepared and available online a week before the semester begins.

It's not a big deal to me since I'm teaching three sections of an American history survey class (beginnings through the Civil War) and one section of an upper-level American Revolution class. Both courses I've taught before, so I just have to tweak my old syllabus and update page numbers to the new editions of the books.

I figure I can get all that done this afternoon and not have to be hassled Monday when my new office mate is going to move in.

I walk the stairs up to the fourth floor—one of the resolutions I make every year to get more exercise that lasts for maybe two weeks—and turn down the hall that leads to a five-office suite that houses three history faculty members, one English professor, and an office for adjunct use.

Now there will be two English faculty in the suite since I'm having to share.

I tell myself to stop whining and focus on the new semester.

I always like the beginning of the term. New courses. New students. A new chance to do better.

A clean slate. An empty page.

This semester is going to be good. I got my classes scheduled the way I like them best, and an annoying person has transitioned off the grievances committee so I won't have to put up with her every month.

Everything will be good.

My office mate will be good.

I don't have anything to complain about.

I'm just starting to believe my pep talk when I reach my office and discover that someone is already in it.

In it.

In my office.

He's reaching up to take one of my framed movie posters off the wall.

I jerk to a stop and stare.

It's Dr. Evan Jones, the new assistant professor in English. I know it's him even though I've never seen him before.

Who else would have barged into my office and started moving stuff around?

The movie posters aren't the only thing he's moved. He's also picked up the throw rug I had near the desk that will be his, and he's moved the three pieces of pottery I had in the second windowsill. He's piled everything neatly on the chair next to my desk.

He turns around, still holding the last framed poster, and sees me in the doorway.

"Good afternoon," he says without a smile.

"Hi." I try to pull myself together. A good first impression will not include a scowl at all my pretty stuff being moved.

Evan is not particularly tall—just four or five inches taller than my five four. He's got a lean, fit build and an upright posture. Very close-cropped dark hair and equally dark eyes. A square jaw. He's wearing neat khakis and a green golf shirt. Tucked in.

He looks around my age. He can't be much older.

He's focused on me but still hasn't smiled.

I've managed to control my immediate resistance to his unexpected presence, and I smile at him. Everyone says I have a good smile. I had a lot of orthodontic work, and I've got dimples on both sides of my mouth. "I thought you wouldn't be here until Monday," I say, pleased that I sound light and natural. "I would have moved my stuff out of your way."

"It's fine," he says, his eyes never leaving my face. "I didn't mind moving it."

Okay then. Definitely not friendly.

I'm not sure what to do, so I walk over to my desk, moving one of the framed posters he's leaned against the side chair to make sure it's stable. I don't like having my rooms messed up. My little house is neat and pretty with everything in its place, and my office was always the same way.

But now he's ransacked it. The empty wall across from my desk glares at me. What if he puts something ugly up and I have to look at it all year long?

What if he doesn't put anything up and I have to look at an empty wall?

I'd been vaguely hoping he was one of those guys like Marcus who doesn't give a second thought to furnishings and would let me leave the office decorated as it was.

Evidently not.

He's standing very straight, still focused on me as I move across the office. He hands me the poster he's still holding.

I take it and lean it against the other two.

I'll have to put them in storage or else find room for them on my side of the office. To do that, I'll need to rearrange everything, but I don't want to do it right now while he's in here being uptight and silent.

Maybe judging me.

When I put down the poster, I realize I haven't even introduced myself. I smile again and step toward him, extending my hand. "I'm sorry I never properly greeted you. I'm Beck Wilson."

"Dr. Wilson," he says soberly. "I'm Evan Jones."

Dr. Wilson? Dr. Wilson? He's calling me Dr. Wilson?

No one but students call me Dr. Wilson, and half of them can barely manage that. Is he really that formal? Is he going to expect me to call him Dr. Jones?

"It's nice to meet you," I tell him, pulling my hand out of his warm, firm grip. "I hope you don't mind sharing an office for a year. They did try very hard to work it out so you could have your own."

"They told me. I'm sure it will be acceptable." He's got the most unnerving look—those dark eyes are so completely unsmiling.

Acceptable. All right then.

"This is a large office for one," he added.

"It is big." My cheeks feel pink. I feel hassled and flustered. I'm normally comfortable around people—even strangers—so I don't know why this man has gotten me totally off stride. "It just happened to be vacant when I started here."

"I see."

I sit down with a flop on my desk chair. I bought it as a present for myself when I first got this job. It's plush and comfortable with good back support and the prettiest shade of rose pink. "So when did you get into town?" I ask. Maybe he's just one of those people who are stiff until they get to know someone. Maybe if I talk to him, he'll loosen up.

"This morning."

"This morning?" I try not to sound too surprised, but

I'm sure my eyes get big. "Didn't you want to get moved in and everything first?"

"I'd rather get moved into my office so I'll be ready to work on Monday." He glances back at the six stacked boxes near the empty bookcases.

There are two bookcases in the office. I was wise enough to know that anyone who moved in would want to use one of the bookcases, so I emptied it early this week. Thank God. Otherwise this man would have piled all my books up on top of my desk.

I clear my throat and try to think of something friendly to say. "Where did you find to live?"

"I'm renting a house on Straight Street. It's just three blocks from campus."

"Oh yeah, you're in my neighborhood then. I'm on Bush. In the little pink house."

The two-bedroom house was pink when I moved in. That's one of the main reasons I bought it. But I can well imagine this guy's response.

He doesn't disappoint. His dark eyebrows go up. "Your house is pink?"

"Yes. Is there something wrong with that?"

"No. You must like pink." His eyes lower to my top, which is dark pink with a scoop neck and three-quarter sleeves. I'm wearing it with a long, casual skirt, and I've pulled the top half of my hair back with a clip and let the rest of it loose. I thought I looked pretty and curvy when I left the house this morning, but I suddenly feel self-conscious.

I push it away immediately. Being a young-looking woman in academia has its challenges, and one of them is that we have to fight for people to respect us and not assume we're silly.

I'm used to surprised, skeptical looks when I introduce myself as a faculty member.

To be fair, Evan doesn't look skeptical or judgmental. He just looks unfriendly.

"I do like pink," I say with another smile, rather forced this time. "So you were at Notre Dame for your PhD?"

"Yes."

"It's a big change, I guess. Moving here to Virginia." I wonder why he took the job at Milford. Notre Dame is a good school, and his publication history is already impressive. Surely he could get a more prestigious job. The job market is tough for faculty in the humanities, but I'd be really surprised if Milford was his only job offer.

"Not really."

That's all he says. *Not really*.

"Where are you from originally?" I ask, still searching for a way to get him to loosen up.

"Virginia."

Oh. Well, that explains it. No wonder he doesn't think moving here is a big transition. "I'm from Virginia too. Farmville," I offer. Some people open up easier if the other person does first. "I did my graduate work at the University of North Carolina."

"I saw that. On your faculty page on the Milford website."

So he's been looking me up. Not surprising. I would have done the same thing. "My folks still live in Farmville. It's nice that they're only a couple of hours away. Is your family still in Virginia?"

"Yes."

"Where in Virginia?"

"Richmond."

"So you're pretty close to them too. That's good."

He doesn't answer. If anything, he looks even more closed up than he did before.

I try not to make a face at him. He's making even simple conversation difficult. "Well, I hope you like it here."

"I'm sure it will be fine." He's still standing, looking at me. It would be more natural if he'd go back to unpacking his boxes, but he doesn't.

I turn on my computer, mostly for something to do. "Well, I'm going to work on a syllabus."

He nods. "I already have mine mostly done."

Of course he does.

Then he adds, "I'd like to know your teaching hours, if I may."

"Excuse me?"

"Your teaching hours? When your classes are? I need to

finalize my office hours, and I'd like to coordinate with your teaching hours if possible."

"Oh." I stare at him, trying to figure out what he's saying. Surely he doesn't think he'll have the office to himself when I'm not teaching. "I'll be in my office at other times too."

"Naturally. But if I schedule my office hours during your teaching hours, we won't be trying to conference with students at the same time."

Conference with students? It's all I can do not to repeat the words back to him. "Oh, um, okay. But students stop by whenever."

"I understand." He doesn't move. He's still waiting.

I manage not to roll my eyes. "This semester, I'm teaching on Mondays, Wednesdays, and Fridays at eight, nine, ten, and one."

For the first time, a real expression crosses his face. It's faint surprise. "You really stack your classes."

"I prefer it that way. The first three are repeats of the same class, so I get into a zone with them. And I prefer to have Tuesdays and Thursdays to focus on my other work."

"I see. That will work fine then. I'll put my office hours on Monday, Wednesday, and Friday mornings. My classes are on Tuesday and Thursday at eight thirty and ten and a Wednesday night class."

He's only teaching three classes? How did he get so lucky?

I've really got to stop acting so petty and thinking the

worst of him. They probably gave him a one-course release because this is his first semester.

He hands me a printed sheet of paper, and I stare down at it in surprise. It's got his teaching and office hours printed out.

"What if I said I was teaching different hours?" I ask.

"I had a couple of other schedules worked out."

Evidently he's one of *those* kinds of people. Always organized. Always planning ahead. Always uptight about even unimportant things.

Just perfect.

Exactly the kind of person who gets annoyed by my personality. He probably already dislikes me.

I thank him for the (unnecessary) printed schedule and turn toward my computer. I've got to adjust dates and page numbers on my syllabus. I've got to change a couple of assignments that didn't work well last time I taught these classes. I need to get ready for a new semester and not worry about my annoying new office mate.

It sounds like we have opposite schedules, so maybe I won't have to sit in the office with him for long periods of time. Maybe he'll make himself scarce.

I'll come in this weekend to rearrange my pretty things on my side of the office. One side will be pretty, and one side will be boring. That much is clear.

I'm not going to worry about it. It's just a year. I can tolerate anything.

I'll keep making a few efforts to be friendly, but if he

doesn't reciprocate, I'm not going to keep running into a brick wall.

He's my office mate. He's not even in my department.

I don't have to like him.

It's a good thing because I already don't.

ON SUNDAY EVENING, I'm taking it easy, texting with Jennifer and flipping through channels on TV.

I've already told her all about Evan, and she's given me some wise, mature advice about not jumping to conclusions and giving him the benefit of the doubt because maybe he's not as uptight and annoying as he seems at first.

I tell her she's right. Because I know she's right. But it's hard for me to feel that she's right. I keep replaying the encounter over and over again in my mind and getting annoyed with him all over again.

I also keep visualizing how good-looking he is and experiencing a deep, physical response to the image.

That annoys me even more.

When another text comes in, I look away from the romantic comedy I've landed on and check my phone. Jennifer says, *I bet he's a nice guy. Maybe he just doesn't make a good first impression.*

Maybe.

Jarissa in Admissions said he helped jump her car on Friday and then followed her home to make sure it didn't stall again. She said he was great.

That was nice.

She thought he was a great guy.

Maybe he liked her more than he liked me.

Why wouldn't he like you?

Don't know.

Give it time.

I will.

I mean what I say. He's evidently a decent guy if he went out of his way to help Jarissa. I usually give people the benefit of the doubt. I'm not sure why I can't seem to give it to Evan.

It doesn't speak well of me. I'm a nicer person than this.

I'm going to do better than this.

Two Towers is on. Faramir scene.

I perk up when Jennifer's text comes in and pull up my cable guide to find the channel. I own the Lord of the Rings movies in three different formats, but that doesn't stop me from watching them when one is running on cable.

It's near the end when I flip over, and I shake my head as I watch the scene where Faramir takes Frodo, Sam, and the ring to Osgiliath, something he never does in the book since his rejection of the temptation of the ring is one of his most worthy characteristics.

After a minute, I text, *Faramir would NEVER do this!*

I know.

NEVER!

I know. You tell me every time.

It needs repeating. A lot! He would NEVER do such a thing! Character assassination!

I know. He's your man. No one is allowed to assassinate his character, not even a movie you love.

I giggle at that because Jennifer knows me so well. *EXACTLY!*

I watch until the end of the movie, and then another text comes in from Jennifer. *So I guess your date last night wasn't Faramir?*

I'd mentioned last night that the date wasn't a success, but I hadn't given her any details. It was a first meeting of a guy I'd connected with through a dating app. I've been trying out different dating apps and online sites since I moved to Milford two years ago. I've met a couple of decent guys—one I dated for three months—but overall there're more losers than winners.

Jennifer knows my favorite male character in The Lord of the Rings is Faramir, and so we use him as a standard for evaluating men.

Definitely not.

I'm pretty sure the guy was disappointed in how I look. I wasn't skinny enough for him. I don't hide my body in the pictures I include, but sometimes guys still expect me to be thinner than I am.

This is an immediate red flag that the guy isn't for me.

I knew from the first minute I met the guy last night

that it was going nowhere. I should have just called it quits right away, but instead we had a quick dinner and went through the motions of the date before we were able to get away.

It wasn't a good evening, but those things happen sometimes when you try to date people you connect with online.

Oh well. Your Faramir is out there somewhere.

I smile at Jennifer's encouraging text. I'm by nature more optimistic than she is, but she's recently fallen in love and gotten engaged to Marcus, so she's predisposed right now to be hopeful about love for other people too. *Maybe. Or maybe he's just in the pages of the book.*

You'll be good either way.

I'll be good either way.

2

Evan listens to opera.

Opera.

I learn this first thing on Monday morning a week later when I get to the office. I arrive at seven forty-five in my usual morning state—which is rushed and slightly frazzled. My hair isn't pulled back yet, and I've got a fistful of jewelry I still need to put on. I'm wearing my favorite dress—it's long and sleeveless in a flattering blue that matches my eyes, and I really like the way it drapes over the curves of my breasts, belly, and hips. Because it's sleeveless, I've paired it with a pretty duster in a gauzy floral fabric. I might not have quite finished dressing, but I still have fifteen minutes before my class starts, and I felt pretty (if a little harried) as I left my house.

Everything changes when I arrive in my office to be

greeted by the sound of opera and Evan typing away at his computer, looking ridiculously handsome in a suit and tie.

A suit.

Plenty of the male professors wear ties to teach—usually paired with old sports jackets and jeans. But the only men at Milford who regularly wear suits are the president and one of the business professors.

But Evan is definitely wearing a real suit. A nice one in charcoal gray with a pale blue shirt and a blue-and-red tie.

He looks like he belongs in a boardroom. Not a Milford classroom.

He also looks so sexy that I actually gulp as my eyes travel up and down his lean body.

I've always thought I'm attracted to laid-back, casual guys, so I don't know why I get this sudden rush of bone-deep attraction.

It doesn't make sense, and it's really annoying since I don't even like this man.

So between the opera and the unexpected surge of lust, my flustered state intensifies. I drop half my jewelry on the floor and stumble over my own feet as I try to make it to my desk.

"Good morning," he says, looking up from his computer at last. Evidently my clumsy route through the office has finally gotten his attention.

"Morning," I say, forcing a smile. I didn't see him much last week since classes hadn't started yet. We had a couple of beginning-of-the-year faculty meetings, but he sat with people from the English department for those. Otherwise, I wasn't in the office much and so I didn't spend much time with him, which I thought was a good transition. I'm over the worst of the annoyance now, and I resolved over the weekend to try to get to know him so I can like him the way I do most people.

"I can turn the music down if you want."

It's not loud, but it's *demanding*, if that makes sense. I'm not opposed to opera in theory, but I never listen to it myself, and it's never struck me as a comfortable background sound. It's so in your face all the time. I don't recognize the opera that's playing, but I'm not all that familiar with the genre, so I probably wouldn't recognize anything except the *Marriage of Figaro*, *Carmen*, or *Pagliacci*.

"It's fine," I tell him. "I have a class at eight anyway."

"That's what I thought." He glances over at the antique-looking clock he's put on his desk. "Are you running late?"

"No." I frown at him, forgetting I'm planning to be nice. "I have fifteen minutes." It's a reminder that I have some things to do before my class begins, so I drop my big leather bag on the floor and go to recover the jewelry that fell as I entered.

I put on my big hoop earrings and bead necklace and then try three times before I can hook my bracelet. I find a brush in my bag and pull it through my hair before I twist it up in a knot.

I usually start the day with my hair pulled back, but it

doesn't last that way for long. It starts to slip out of any clip I use, and I'm too busy with other things to mess with it.

Evan watches me, and I have no idea what he's thinking.

Surely he doesn't mind my doing my hair in my own office. If he does, he'll have to get used to it. I also freshen up my makeup at my desk after lunch.

"What time did you get in?" I ask him, searching for easy conversation.

"Six thirty."

"Six thirty? Do you always get up that early, or was it just because it's your first day?"

"I usually get up at five. I work out for an hour, and then I get dressed and am ready for work." He says this as if it's a normal daily schedule, when I know maybe two other people at Milford who regularly work out before coming to campus.

Quite a few of the faculty are in good shape, but they don't get their exercise done at ungodly early hours of the morning. A lot of them don't even show up until lunchtime, depending on when their classes are scheduled.

"Oh," I say. "I'm still sleeping at that time."

"What time do you go to bed? If you'd go to bed earlier, you could get up earlier."

I manage not to roll my eyes at this piece of advice. "I'm sure that's true," I murmur, avoiding his eyes so he won't see my response. I find the books I need for the course and grab the notebook I put together last week for my survey classes.

I glance in the mirror. I look nice. Soft and curvy and feminine and basically pulled together.

I'm sure my particular brand of looks isn't what does it for Evan. I'm sure he likes slim, polished women. But that doesn't matter. I used to be self-conscious about being bigger than normal, and for years I tried to lose some weight so I could get down to what is considered average sized. But sometime in the past five years, I grew to accept my body with all its curves and roundness. Plenty of guys like how I look, and I'm usually perfectly happy with it. I'm certainly not going to let Evan's cool regard make me feel bad about myself. Despite that weird attraction I felt earlier, I couldn't care less if he likes how I look.

"Okay," I say after I've confirmed that I don't have a smear of mascara under my eye or too much cleavage showing. "I'm off."

"Have a good class."

Just in case I haven't been clear, he still hasn't smiled. Not today. And not at me ever.

It's the weirdest thing.

Surely even serial killers smile occasionally.

I brush away the thought of Evan so I can focus on my classes. For the next three hours, I hardly think about him at all.

Since I have only ten minutes between my first three classes, I don't get back to the office until a little after eleven. I'm on that teaching high I get when a class goes well. I feel like I was articulate and insightful, and I got good responses from students.

I've chatted with four people on my way back to the office, so I'm in a good mood when I walk in the door.

Evan is still at his desk, typing on his computer, wearing his suit, and listening to opera.

I wonder if he's gotten up even once the whole time I was gone.

Maybe he has an iron bladder and doesn't feel the need to get up and wander around every hour or so to talk to people like I do.

I give him a cheerful hello, resolving yet again to be nice to him. I'll feel a lot more comfortable with this situation if we can at least get along.

He murmurs a response and doesn't look up from his computer monitor.

I try not to scowl.

I redid the wall hangings and decorations on my side of the office to make room for the ones he rejected. I notice that one of my framed posters is tilted askew, so I pause to straighten it.

"Why The Lord of the Rings?" he asks.

I hadn't realized he'd deigned to look away from his computer, but evidently he has since he's asking about the posters. The three movie posters are the three Lord of the

Rings movies. The first one showing the boats on the river at the Argonath, the next of Orthanc and Barad-dûr with a lot of atmospheric smoke between them, and the last one of Aragorn and his sword.

"Don't you like The Lord of the Rings?" I ask, turning around, genuinely interested.

"I love the books."

"Oh. I love the books too. But I also love the movies." I'm doing my best to keep my resolve of friendliness, but he seems to invariably trigger my annoyance button, which almost never gets pushed by anyone else. "Do you not like the movies?"

"I've never seen them." He's turned his chair away from his computer to face me, so at least that's a sign he's involved in the conversation.

"Seriously? You haven't seen the Lord of the Rings movies?"

He shook his head. "I didn't think I'd like them. Aren't they just elves doing backflips?"

I almost choke. "No! They're not just elves doing backflips. I can't believe you really haven't seen them."

"You like them that much?"

"Yes. They're not perfect movies, but they're really quite good. I don't know. The first one came out when I was twelve or thirteen. I'd just read the books for the first time, and I was totally consumed by the movies. I think it was just a pivotal time for me. I really got into them. That's when I got the posters—when the movies first came out." I swallow, realizing I'm probably oversharing and he might not want to hear all this. "They... they spoke to me. So, anyway, the posters mean a lot to me now because they meant so much to me back then." I drop my eyes. "If that makes sense."

"It does," he murmurs.

What is this? Is he actually interested? Is he understanding something I'm trying to express?

"The score is really over the top, isn't it?"

Okay. Maybe I was wrong. "Over the top?" I ask coolly.

"Over-the-top emotional. I've heard parts of it."

"It's a movie score. The whole point of it is to evoke emotion. What else is it supposed to do?"

He tilts his head slightly. I might be wrong, but I could swear the corners of his mouth twitch up just a little.

Is it a smile? *Now*?

Is he trying to rile me up on purpose or something?

I don't get this guy at all.

I narrow my eyes. "And anyone who listens to opera shouldn't be criticizing other kinds of music for being too emotional."

I didn't miss it this time. His mouth twitches up so quickly it's almost imperceptible. "Fair enough."

Maybe I should consider it a victory. That I nearly got him to smile.

And I would be glad about it if I didn't suspect he was mostly just laughing at me.

Office Mate

FOR THE NEXT THREE WEEKS, there isn't much improvement in our office cohabitation.

We do get into a pattern. We go through regular small talk and learn to stay out of each other's way. We sometimes talk when we're in the office together for long periods of time, but it's always similarly awkward discussions. I never know what he's thinking, and I'm convinced he doesn't even like me.

I know he can talk. And he can smile and laugh. I know this only because I've caught him occasionally having discussions with other faculty members, usually talking about research interests or literature.

But he never talks like that with me. He definitely never laughs.

He probably thinks I'm silly, frivolous, girly, insubstantial, and every other negative impression people have always had about me.

I try not to worry about it, but it bothers me.

A lot.

On a Thursday a few weeks after the term started, I'm trying to type up the minutes for a committee meeting I just attended. (I unfortunately ended up being nominated as secretary.) Evan comes back from his second class at a little before noon, and he's got three students in tow.

Two girls and a boy.

They evidently all have questions for him about papers

they're writing, and he talks to them each in turn. He's very serious and gentle in his discussions with them, taking time to make sure they understand and asking them insightful questions.

He might not smile and laugh a lot, but he's good with students.

And he doesn't even seem to notice that both the girls are making goo-goo eyes at him.

It's not surprising. He's young and good-looking and unmarried. Of course students are into him.

It's not a big deal. It's another thing that shouldn't bother me but does.

I keep working on the minutes as he meets with the students, but I don't focus very well since I keep listening in to the conversations.

He looks as handsome as ever today in one of his suits. He's got five of them, and he wears one each day. I've kept track, so I know this for sure. He doesn't always wear them in the same order or on the same days, but he wears each suit once a week, and he only has five.

When the last student leaves, he goes to the bathroom (I assume that's where he goes, although obviously I'm not there to witness it) and comes back to pull his lunch out.

He usually brings his lunch. Either a sandwich and a piece of fruit or leftovers from whatever he had for dinner last night. Today he has a turkey sandwich, an apple, and water in the refillable bottle he always uses.

It might be healthy, but it sounds quite unappetizing to me.

I'm trying to finish these stupid minutes so I can go to the dining hall to get something to eat and then head to the library to talk to one of the librarians about coming to my classes and talking about library research. I've got another committee meeting late this afternoon, and I want to get everything done before then.

"What are you working on?" Evan asks without warning, just before taking a bite of his apple.

I turn in surprise. He usually doesn't volunteer conversation. "Just writing up minutes for the meeting I had earlier. Irritating but necessary."

"Ah."

I don't have to ask what he's going to be working on. He prepares his lesson plans for the entire week on Monday so he can spend the rest of his spare time on his writing. "How's your book coming?"

He's got a contract from a reputable university press to turn his dissertation into a book. It comes as no surprise to me that he's already got a book on his vita. He's an overachiever if there ever was one, and he doesn't seem to do anything except work.

"Good. Just finishing the second chapter."

"That's good." I try to think of an intelligent question to ask about John Milton, but I can't think of anything.

I think the conversation is about to end, but he finishes

chewing his bite and then says, "I see you did some work on Anne Bradstreet in your dissertation."

My eyes widen. "Where did you see that?"

"I looked it up." He clears his throat. "I was curious about your scholarship."

Hopefully he wasn't dubious about my ability to do good scholarship, but it's impossible to tell from his face. "Oh."

"I would be interested in hearing about it."

"About Anne Bradstreet?"

"About your dissertation."

"Oh. Okay. Sure." I'm confused and strangely flustered. Don't ask me why. I just am. "If you want."

"Perhaps we can talk about it sometime when you're not busy?"

This is strange. It feels significant, but I have no idea why. He's just so serious about it. And it's small talk. He can't be all that interested in my dissertation on women's concept of history in colonial America. It has absolutely nothing to do with his areas of research or teaching. He's probably just being polite, and it's a nice gesture. Maybe it's a good sign, but I wish he would approach it more casually. "Sure," I say with a bland smile, turning back to my committee notes since I feel so weird and self-conscious. "That would be fine."

"Good." He goes back to work too, and neither of us talk until I finish writing up the minutes and get up to go to lunch and escape the office for a little while.

Office Mate

I WORK LATER than normal that evening because my four-o'clock meeting runs long.

It's almost five thirty when I start walking home. (I wisely had thought to bring my bag with me so I don't have to stop by the office before I head back to my house.)

Because my house is so close to the college, I walk unless the weather is bad. The campus is surrounded by an established residential neighborhood, most of the houses small and built in the forties and fifties. I've crossed the street that's one of the boundaries of the campus and am walking down a sidewalk when I pass a vacant lot.

The property belongs to the adjoining house, but they've never used it, so it's been nothing but grass since I've moved here.

A figure in the grass catches my attention.

Kids will sometimes play in the lot, but that is not a kid. It's a man in a suit.

A second look proves why the figure seemed familiar at first glance.

It's Evan.

He's crouching down in the middle of the lot. I have no idea what he's doing.

"What are you doing?" I call out.

He jerks in surprise and stands up. A quick expression twists on his face, and it's so quick I'm not positive what it is.

Maybe he doesn't want to see me. Or maybe he's embarrassed.

What the hell was he doing?

I stand and wait until he comes over to me. "Hey," he says. "You're heading home later than normal today."

I frown at him. "I had a late meeting. What were you doing?"

He lets out a breath that sounds resigned. "I was..." He clears his throat and shows me something in his hand. It's a broken silver barrette. "I was picking this up."

"Why were you picking up the barrette? Do you go around picking up trash?"

"No." He glances over at the lot and then back at me. "Okay, fine. I leave peanuts there for a couple of crows every morning, and they leave me shiny things as a thank-you. I pick them up on my way home so they won't think I'm rejecting their gifts."

My eyes widen, and my breath hitches in my throat. "What?"

"You heard me."

"You leave peanuts for crows?" I don't know why this piece of information excites me, but it does. My heart has sped up. My stomach has gotten flutters.

"Yeah." He gives me a sheepish look. He's obviously a little embarrassed by admitting that to me. "I was eating some one Saturday as I walked over to campus, and I saw the crows looking for food in the lot, so I tossed the leftover peanuts to them. They were waiting for me the next day to see if I had more peanuts, so I started taking a few with me to toss to them. Now they're there every morning waiting for their peanuts."

I cover my mouth with one hand as if this might hold back a swell of feeling. "That's so sweet."

"It's not a big deal. They're just peanuts. But they've started leaving me things, so I try to pick them up as I go home."

"I had no idea crows would do that!"

"They're pretty smart. If you're mean to them, they'll hold a grudge and tell all their buddies about you. But if you're nice to them, they'll try to thank you as best they can."

"I love that." I've still got that pressure of emotion in my chest and the butterflies in my stomach. It's a swoony kind of feeling I really shouldn't be feeling about Evan. "I had no idea."

He gives me a little smile. It's very small—barely a smile at all—but I see it. No way I would miss it. "It's not a big deal."

It feels like a big deal to me, but I don't want to embarrass him by acting like the small gesture is important.

But it tells me something new about Evan.

He has a kind heart—even for animals that other people don't care about.

There's a lot more to him than I had realized at first.

A WEEK later Evan brings up my dissertation again. He wants to talk about it with me.

I don't know about everyone else, but I didn't actually love my dissertation. I think some parts of it were good. I got two articles out of it and a few conference papers. Since Milford isn't a research-focused college, that's more than enough for the administration to be happy with my research output. But I don't think overall my dissertation is all that great. I wrote some of it just to get it done. And it was such a stressful time of my life that I don't much like to think about it now.

Mostly I've moved on. I'm two years out of my PhD program now, so not very many people even ask me about it anymore.

But Evan, evidently determined to always be contrary, wants to talk about it with me, and there's no way I can politely put it off.

Jennifer keeps telling me it's a good thing. He's showing some interest in me. He wants to get to know me better. He wants to be on better terms, just like I do.

But surely he could do that by talking about movies or books we both like or our families or places we've traveled or hobbies we have or the crows he gives peanuts to or anything except my dissertation.

But no. It's only the dissertation he wants to hear about.

And when I tell him I'll be happy to talk one afternoon, he suggests we go get coffee.

Which means I'll be stuck with him for at least a half hour, talking about my dissertation.

I hate the thought of the stupid thing.

He suggests a coffee shop just a block from campus, and I'm relieved because I don't want everyone on campus to see us in the dining hall together and start to get ideas.

I make conversation about the neighborhood as we walk, relieved I wore comfortable shoes today with my tunic top and broomstick skirt. It's a warm day, and I'm perspiring a little when we get there. Hopefully I won't perspire off all my makeup or sweat through my top.

We get our coffee—mine is actually hot chocolate since I don't like drinking coffee in the afternoon—and he pays for both drinks. We find a table for two in one corner. It's not that crowded in late afternoon, and I don't see anyone from Milford.

I'm not sure why I'm worried about it. It's just that I can imagine Evan's face if people started talking about us, wondering if we're dating or something.

He wouldn't like that at all.

"So," I say, trying to relax and find my normal friendly attitude. "You wanted to talk about my dissertation?"

"Yes."

He starts quizzing me.

Seriously.

It feels like an oral exam.

He doesn't just want to hear about the broad strokes, the normal summary I share with anyone who happens to ask. He wants details. And some of those details I haven't thought about in more than two years.

I can't remember everything, and I have to struggle to keep up with his queries.

It's exhausting, and I really have no idea why he wants to know so much about such a random topic.

But I do my best. I wouldn't be rude to him anyway, and I'm hoping it's progress that he wants to talk to me at all.

He questions me for over an hour. He's really incredibly smart. He pulls together my ideas in ways I hadn't realized they'd fit together. It makes my dissertation sound better than I think it actually was.

At least he comes away with a positive impression of it, whether it's based in reality or not. And I'm relieved when he finally runs out of questions.

I wonder what he'd be like on a date. Would he approach his date with the same kind of studious reserve? Would he question her like he was giving an exam?

The thought tickles my humor, and I have to struggle not to giggle.

"What is it?" Evan asks, his dark eyes searching my face.

"Nothing."

"You were laughing."

"I wasn't either."

"You were trying not to. Did I do something funny?"

"No. Not at all." That much is definitely the truth. In

the month I've known him, he hasn't made a single joke and he's never laughed out loud.

"Then what were you laughing at?"

I shake my head. I'm generally an honest, open person without a lot of qualms about sharing my personal stuff, but there's no way I can tell him the truth that I was giggling about how he'd act on a date. "It's really nothing. I'm just surprised you're so interested in my dissertation."

"There's a lot of overlap in our topics—John Milton was a Puritan, you know."

"Of course he was." I honestly hadn't even thought about it. Maybe that explains his incongruous interest. "Do you see a lot of common themes?"

He nods. "Theologically, absolutely. Socially, some. Politically, not nearly as much."

"Well, I'll read your book when you have it done so I can see any similarities between our work." I smile at him, feeling a little better now that I have a context for his interest.

"Will you?"

"Of course. Why wouldn't I?"

"It's not the kind of book most people would read for general interest."

I shrug. "Well, I'll read it anyway."

"You can read the chapters I have done now if you'd like." He's been looking down at his coffee cup, but he slants a look up at my face through his thick lashes. I have no idea what he's looking for in my face.

I'm surprised, but I immediately recognize that it will be easier to read a dense tome in chapters than all in one fell swoop. "Sure. I'll read them anytime."

"I'll send them to you when I get back to my computer."

He's really taking this seriously. Hopefully he won't expect brilliant insights. I'm as smart as anyone, and I have a really good knowledge of American history. But my intelligence works by intuitively understanding cycles and cultural moments and the development of thought and action. I always feel out of my depth when people dive deep into critical theory. It just doesn't fit with how I understand my field.

I smile, however, since I figure we've made progress today. "That would be great. I can read them this weekend."

"I'd love to hear what you think."

"Okay. Sure."

I'm relieved when we get up to leave. We walk back to campus together, and Evan is very quiet.

Not that that's unusual.

We reach our office, and we both stand there inside the door. I'm not sure why. It's just that neither of us move. We look at each other, and I'm hit again with another one of those waves of attraction.

He really is unjustly good-looking. I really like the square lines of his face. How deep his eyes are—like they're full of thoughts he never shares. I like the solid line of his shoulders under his suit jacket. I like how I have to look up to him, but he's not so tall that it feels like he's on a different floor of the building.

My skin flushes, and a pressure clenches in my chest, between my legs.

It's the most ridiculous thing, but I really want to touch him. I want him to touch me. He's got really good hands. Lean and graceful.

I imagine those hands touching me. Those eyes looking down on me in bed.

That body without any clothes.

I swallow hard.

"Thank you for talking to me," he says. Jennifer was right from the beginning. The man is very polite.

"You're welcome. I'm glad you were interested."

"I'll send you those chapters."

"I'll read them this weekend." I clench my hands at my sides. I'm not going to touch him, no matter how much I want to. I really want to take the lapels of his jacket in my hands. I want to stroke his short hair with my fingers.

What the hell is wrong with me?

He sniffs and shifts from foot to foot. "Good."

"Good."

"Good."

This is ridiculous. One of us needs to move. It's going to be me. Otherwise, I'm going to humiliate myself by hauling the man down into a kiss. "Okay," I say brightly. "I think I'm going to head home to grade papers."

"Sounds like a plan."

He still doesn't move, so I do. I stumble over to my desk, throw my stuff into my bag, and turn off my computer.

He's still standing in the same place, looking at me when I hook my bag strap over my shoulder.

"I'll see you tomorrow," I say.

"Goodbye, Beck."

Shit. I love how he just said my name.

I want him to say it again.

And that's the very last straw.

I get out of the office as fast as I can.

3

The following Tuesday, I come into campus at around nine thirty. Since I don't teach on Tuesdays and Thursdays, I don't feel a great need to get to the office at the crack of dawn.

I stop by the financial aid office to say hello to Jennifer since she didn't answer my text last night and I want to make sure she's doing all right.

"Hey," she says as soon as she sees me. She's standing up at her desk, searching through a pile of files. "Sorry I never answered."

"It's fine. I know you have things that occupy your time." I cause my voice to lilt slightly so it's clear what I'm teasingly referring to.

Jennifer snorts. "It wasn't *that*. Marcus didn't actually come over last night at all. He was helping his dad on the farm, and I was with Grandma all evening."

My smile fades. "Is she okay?" Jennifer's grandmother had a major stroke two years ago, and she's in a nursing home now. Jennifer visits her faithfully.

"She had a bad day, but she's hanging in there." Jennifer's expression changes, softening into a smile. "So how are things in the office?"

I shake my head and roll my eyes. "Okay, I guess. As okay as they're going to be."

"Did he interrogate you on the chapters of his book you read over the weekend?"

"Oh yes. First thing yesterday morning." I giggle as I recall his studious expression as I gave him my thoughts. "He took notes."

"He did not!" Jennifer laughs with me. "I kind of like this guy."

"You don't even know him."

"I know him through you. And he's my kind of guy. He works hard and takes things seriously and doesn't mess around. You should get along with him well since you've had so much practice with me."

"But I know what you're thinking most of the time. I have no idea about him. The man has walls a mile high and half a mile thick. It's frustrating."

"Surely he's not that bad. You're only annoyed right now because he quizzed you on your dissertation last week, and you don't like thinking about it. You seemed to be getting used to him before that."

"Maybe." I think through what she said and decide

she's probably right. "It was downright painful, let me tell you. I was so uncomfortable."

"I've been thinking about it," Jennifer says, lowering her voice although we're alone in her office. "And I wonder if he maybe thought it was a date."

I almost choke. "What? No way!"

"Are you sure? He made a point of asking you, and he went off campus and he bought your coffee."

"Guys don't go on dates like that and then interrogate girls on their dissertation!" I'm blushing, and I have no idea why. I'm usually not particularly embarrassed about talking about men. Even men I like (and I don't like Evan much at all!).

"How do you know how he dates? Maybe he's socially awkward and the only way he can relate is talking about scholarship."

This gives me pause since I haven't thought about it before. But then I shake my head firmly. "No. No way. I'd know if he was even remotely interested."

"Like I knew with Marcus?"

I've been holding my bag, but it's full of books and getting heavy, so I drop it to the floor. I count off on my fingers as I reply, "First off, you were blind with Marcus. I could tell he was interested. Everyone could tell he was interested. Only you couldn't." Before Jennifer can object to this, I continue, "Second of all, Marcus kissed you. That was a sign even if nothing else was. Evan hasn't even shaken my hand since the first time I met him. Thirdly, I'm not his type at all. I'm sure he's looking for a serious, uptight, buttoned-up girl who will match him. Fourthly, you've never seen him around me, so you have absolutely no way to judge. Fifthly... well, I can't think of a fifth point, but I don't need one. The first four should be convincing enough."

Jennifer's laughing softly. "Fine, fine. I'm really just teasing you. But I won't do it anymore if you're going to be so sensitive about it."

"I'm not sensitive!" I don't know why I get defensive, but I do. I'm usually pretty easygoing about teasing. It doesn't bother me.

Jennifer raises her eyebrows. "Okay. You're not sensitive."

"Well, I'm not normally sensitive. I don't know what's the matter with me. I'm just used to feeling settled in my own skin and comfortable around other people, and he disturbs me for some reason."

Jennifer seems to be hiding a particular expression.

"Not for the reasons you're thinking," I insist.

"Of course not. Who'd want a boyfriend who does nothing but ask about your dissertation?"

That makes me laugh, and I feel better after that.

FOR THE NEXT TWO WEEKS, Evan and I fall into a pattern of interacting in the office that seems to work. We talk about our work and our classes. I avoid asking him any personal questions since when I do he clams up. The only personal thing I learn from him is that he drives out to Richmond every Saturday to have lunch with his younger sister, who is evidently still in high school. I'm not sure why he has lunch with his sister and not his parents, but it's clear from his expression that he doesn't want to answer questions like that, so I don't ask.

Otherwise, I try to avoid overly personal questions. We don't try to make conversation all the time, which helps take off some of the pressure.

And a couple of times Evan even smiles at something I say.

It's improvement. I'll take it. If it keeps up like this, then I'll be able to make it through the year with him as my office mate.

On a Sunday evening in October, I decide to take a walk.

If it's not clear by now, I'm not big on exercise. I hate gyms, and my body isn't built for running, and there's no conveniently located pool for me to swim laps. But I do walk fairly regularly—usually a couple of miles. Occasionally I get involved in planning out a paper or a lesson plan in my head and forget how far I walk. On Sunday, I'm thinking through possible topics of conversation with Evan, and I end up walking more than two miles before I think about turning around.

Despite my size, I'm in decent condition. I can walk five

miles without collapsing. But it isn't easy for me, and I hadn't been planning to do that this evening. I'm annoyed with myself as I turn around for the long walk home.

And annoyed with Evan. It feels like this might be partly his fault.

I recognize the injustice of this, but it's not an easy feeling to fight.

It's a long walk and a tiring one. I'm drenched in sweat when I get back to my neighborhood since Octobers are still warm and humid in this part of Virginia. I'm sure my face is beet red, and my hair is all coming out of the braid I tried to contain it in. Hopefully I can make it home before I run into anyone I know. I particularly don't want to see any of my students.

There's someone else I'd rather not see, and he's exactly the person I do see.

Dr. Evan Jones.

I don't recognize him at first because he's on a bike—a nice one by the looks of it—and is wearing a helmet. But he pulls to a stop on the road beside me and I blink at him in confusion, wiping sweat away from my eyes with the back of my hands.

He takes off his helmet to reveal his handsome face. His cheeks are flushed from the wind, and his skin is slightly damp from perspiration. (Not nearly as sweaty as me.) He's wearing shorts and a T-shirt, and I've never seen him look so casual before.

I gulp as I see him. My legs are already weak from exertion, and they wobble dangerously as I process a wave of raw attraction. I've only ever seen him in suits.

I've never seen him like this.

He looks less defended somehow. Like he's a real person.

A person I really want to touch.

"Good evening," he says. I have no idea if he's happy to see me, unless the small tilt of his mouth is a smile.

"Hi," I manage to gasp.

I really, really, really wish I wasn't so hot and sweaty and sloppy right now.

I pull my T-shirt away from my skin since it's sticking from all my sweat. "It's hotter than I realized," I say, hoping to explain away the state I'm in.

"It is." He's still astride his bike but not on the seat. Both his feet are on the pavement. His brown eyes are running up and down my body—my bare legs, my hips, my shirt clinging to the heavy curves of my breasts and belly—and there's a new look in his eyes.

I'm not sure what it is, but it makes my skin flush even hotter. In another man, I'd say it was lust, but that can't be right. Not with Evan. Not with the mess I am right now.

He's probably surprised to see me exercising.

"Do you walk a lot?" he asks, after we stare at each other in silence for too long.

I shrug. "I walk most days but not this much. I went farther than I realized." I look down at the ground before I tell myself I have no reason to feel self-conscious. "How often do you ride?"

"Not as often as I'd like."

I know from what he's told me that he works out at a gym every morning, so he must save the bike rides for evenings and weekends. "I haven't ridden a bike in ages."

He cocks his head. "You want to try?"

"No, I don't want to try!"

"Why not?"

"Because I'll probably fall over and wreck your pretty bike."

He chuckles. It's a real laugh. It might be the first time I've ever heard one from him. "You're not going to wreck my bike." He swings a leg over so he's standing next to it, holding it upright. "Get on and give it a try."

I experience a moment of panic—the kind I feel when I'm trapped in a situation I don't want to be in. I absolutely do not want to ride his bike. I can't imagine myself doing it. But he's being nice right now, and I don't want to throw it back in his face.

And I also don't want him to think I'm unable to do something so simple.

So I take the handles he offers me and silently pray I'm not about to make a fool of myself.

I feel off-balance and awkward as I try to get into the seat and position my feet on the pedals. He reaches over to help me, so his hands end up on my body. One on my shoulder and one on my hips, very close to my bottom.

I really like how they feel, and it gets me even more confused and fluttery. When I start to pedal, I wobble back and forth dangerously.

He laughs and reaches to stabilize the bike.

"I can do it," I gasp. "I told you it's been a while."

"Do you want me to run beside you and hold it upright like a kid off training wheels?"

I suck in an indignant breath and flash my eyes over to him. Then I realize he's teasing me.

Teasing.

Dr. Evan Jones.

Teasing me.

I give him an exaggerated huff and try again. This time I keep my balance and I'm able to make the bike move. It's not comfortable. The bike is large and not made for a woman. But I make it down the block, do a U-turn, and ride back to him.

Figuring I've done enough to prove myself, I'm finally allowed to get off.

"Good job," he says with a smile. It changes his whole face. His eyes warm and soften.

I can't look away. I do manage to swing my leg over the seat and hand the bike to him. "I can't believe I still know how to do it."

"You know what they say," Evan says soberly, his voice slightly thick. "Riding a bike is like... riding a bike."

He made a joke!

"You made a joke!"

I've never been good at keeping my feelings to myself.

He frowns at me. "Why are you surprised?"

"Because you've never made a joke before."

"I haven't?" He's totally serious. I can see that for sure.

"No! I didn't know you ever did."

"Well, I do. Occasionally." He smiles at me again.

I smile back like a dope.

We smile at each other for way too long, and I'm hit with that wave of attraction again—made even stronger because it feels like I really know him for the first time.

"Well," he says.

"Well." I wipe some more sweat from my face with the back of one forearm. I hope I don't look too terrible.

"Well," he repeats. He wipes some sweat away too, but he uses the bottom of his T-shirt. It exposes an expanse of firm, flat belly and a trail of dark hair leading under the waistband of his shorts.

The sight nearly knocks me off my feet, and the surge of lust terrifies me so much I make a quick escape. "Okay. I'll see you tomorrow morning," I tell him, trying to smile naturally. "Thanks for letting me try your bike."

He stands without moving. "You're welcome."

Our eyes meet again before I make myself turn away. I walk in the direction of my house. I don't look back, but I'm sure he's still standing there.

Watching me walk away.

THE FOLLOWING morning I have no idea what to expect when I get to the office.

I tossed and turned way too long during the night, thinking about Evan, imagining myself kissing him, touching him, having sex with him. It was a highly disturbing state of mind, but I couldn't talk myself out of it.

So I'm tense and jittery as I hurry to campus on Monday morning, just in time for my eight-o'clock class.

Evan is in the office already as usual, working on his lesson plans in one of his suits.

"Good morning," he says, giving me a little smile.

I'm so surprised by the expression that I jerk to a stop, smiling back. "Hi."

"I hope you enjoyed your walk last night."

"I did. I'm sore this morning though. I walked too long." I'm about to say something else when I remember the time. "I've got class in five minutes!"

"I know. You better get going."

I put on my jewelry and knot up my hair as fast as I can. Then I grab my books and run for the door.

I wish I could talk to Evan more. I like the mood he's in right now.

But I have class, so I don't have time for anything else.

Maybe we can pick up our discussion again later today.

I RETURN to the office a little after eleven, having finished my three classes in a row.

I've been distracted all morning with thoughts about Evan. I'm not normally like this, so I don't know why I'm all uptight about him.

Yes, he's attractive. And yes, he's like a challenge. But that doesn't explain why I can't get him out of my mind.

When I get there, he's busy at his computer. He murmurs a hello but doesn't turn around to talk to me.

I stare at his back for a minute before I put down my books.

Well, fine. If that's how he wants to act.

I don't need to talk to him either.

I'm feeling ridiculously huffy, and even though I know it's silly and irrational, I can't talk myself out of the feeling.

He's working. It's a Monday morning. Of course he needs to focus on his work and not on me.

I'm not sure why I expected anything else.

I'M FEELING grumpy the next day. Partly because I'm disappointed about Evan (even knowing I don't have any reason for it). And partly because I have three classes of papers to grade.

I'm determined to get through them all today. They're the first short paper in the semester, so they're not very long, and I don't have anything else scheduled all day.

But grading papers is my least favorite part of my job (other than endless, pointless committee meetings), and I'm out of sorts all day.

I do okay in the morning. Evan is out of the office because he teaches two classes today, and I force myself to plug through paper after paper. Many of them rushed and thrown together. Most of them boring. Only a few of them good.

A normal batch of sophomore history papers.

But Evan returns to the office at lunchtime. He didn't talk to me much yesterday, aside from the brief conversation in the morning, and I haven't seen him yet today since he didn't come back to the office between his classes.

"Hey," I say, staying focused on my computer. I do all my grading in Track Changes and comments in the Word documents students submit.

"Hello. How are you?"

"Grading papers."

"I'm sorry."

"Me too. I've got seventy-eight of them."

"Ugh. You should stagger the due dates so you don't get them in from three classes at the same time."

"It's too hard to do that. It messes up the rhythm of my schedule. I prefer to have all my classes doing the same thing at the same time."

"I understand, but you could easily make the assignment due dates different while still—"

"I'm not a newbie," I interrupt, so hassled I don't guard

my words as I normally do with Evan. "I know how to teach and how to plan a syllabus."

He doesn't respond, and the silence feels full.

"Sorry," I say, turning to look at his sober face. "I know you were trying to help." My words are mollifying, but I don't feel very good-natured.

It's just one of those days when I'm frustrated with the world, and Evan is the most annoying thing in it.

"I was. And I still think seventy-eight papers is a ridiculous number to try to grade at the same time. You really don't want to—"

"No!" I've given up being reasonable. I turn in my chair and scowl at him. "I know how to teach. I know what I'm doing. You're not smarter than me. Maybe I like movies and pretty things, but that doesn't mean I'm not serious or smart."

I've clearly surprised him because his lips part as he stares at me. "I never said you weren't."

"Well, you act like it." Then my innate sense of justice kicks in, so I qualify the statement. "Sometimes. I'm a competent adult who's good at my job. I know how to plan a schedule and assign due dates that work for me. I don't need you to tell me what to do."

Something is changing on his face. It's tightening. I think, for the very first time, he might be getting angry. "I never once implied that you don't," he grits out. He's breathing more heavily. "And I don't appreciate your acting like I'm belittling you when I'm not."

"And I don't appreciate all your sober, condescending looks all the time. You could smile a little, you know. You could make small talk."

His eyes narrow. "And you could not run away whenever we start to have a real conversation."

I gape. "What? I never run away."

"Don't you?" His voice is dry, slightly bitter.

He's angry. Not hot and explosive, but definitely angry.

And for some reason it's making me hot.

Hot in a very particular way.

What the hell? This is ridiculous. Having this annoying argument shouldn't be making me all lustful.

The fact that it does enrages me even more. "I don't. I've tried for almost two months to get to know you, and you're the one who refuses to talk about anything but work. So don't you dare act like it's my fault we've never gotten along. You're the one who never smiles. And you're the one who is always looking down on me for things you think are feminine or not serious enough. And you're the one who doesn't know how to relax. This... this... this..." I'm at a loss for words, so I gesture between us to indicate our situation. "This is more your fault than mine."

I stare at him, flushed and panting, and he just stares back. He doesn't reply. He doesn't move.

And I still—still—have no idea what he's thinking.

I make an exasperated sound in my throat and save the document I've been working on. Then I get up, grab my purse, and leave before I explode and say something truly embarrassing.

Or do something.

Let him know that, despite my annoyance with him and his habits, I'm still having trouble keeping my hands off him.

The whole situation is enraging.

And I still have forty-one more papers to grade today.

I GO to the library since I find it a comforting space, and Jennifer is in a meeting so I can't rant to her. I wander around the stacks for a while, go to the bathroom, and talk to a student I find studying in one of the easy chairs.

After that, I've settled down, and I start to feel kind of stupid for my storm of feeling.

Nothing that happened justified getting so upset.

Evan just unsettles me.

And now he probably thinks I'm even sillier than he thought before.

I'm leaving the library when I run into Katrina Pierce, who's one of the research librarians and started working at Milford at the same time I did. She's tiny and a lot like a Disney fairy with pale blond hair and violet-blue eyes, but she also has a competent, no-nonsense attitude I've always liked. I smile and wave, and she stops to chat with me for a minute.

"Did you get what you need?" she asks, glancing down at my hands and seeing that I'm not carrying any books.

"I didn't really need anything. I just wanted to stretch my legs and get some fresh air."

She's got thick, dark lashes. They narrow with skeptical scrutiny. "In the library?"

I laugh. "Well, you know. I find the smell of books very refreshing. Mostly I just wanted to get out of my office for a while. I've got tons of papers to grade."

"Ah. I get it now." She pauses briefly. "You're sharing offices with that Jones guy this year, aren't you?"

"Yeah. Yeah, I am."

"How's that going? I find him rather intimidating. Is he as brilliant as he seems?"

"Well, yeah, he's pretty darn smart. He's a good teacher though. Students seem to like him a lot. He's not over their heads all the time. He's..." I trail off, realizing I'm starting to babble out compliments, and I don't want Katrina to get the wrong impression.

She laughs. "I guess you like him then."

"Oh. Yeah. Sure." I'm embarrassed and also embarrassed about being embarrassed. "He's kind of hard to get to know, I guess."

"Is he shy? He's always been quiet when I see him around."

"I don't think he's shy. At least he doesn't act shy. He's just..." I don't finish the thought. I like Katrina and would consider her a friend, but I'm not going to go around bad-mouthing my office mate to people on campus. "He's very nice."

Katrina's eyebrows pull together. "Is there something going on?"

"No! Of course not."

"Because you're acting kind of... strange." Katrina's expression is amused and sympathetic, and so I'm not offended by the intrusive questioning.

I groan and tug on my braid. "I know. It's just been kind of weird. He's very nice and has never done anything that's a problem. I'm just used to getting along with people better than I have with him."

"It takes some people longer to warm up. Maybe he's one of them."

"Yeah. Yeah, you're probably right."

"He was saying all kinds of nice things about you the other day."

I blink. "He was what?"

"One day last week. He was in here with Jeff Bryson, and I overheard some of their conversation. He was talking about how smart you were and how much students love you and how you had a really insightful dissertation."

My cheeks flush, and my heartbeat speeds up. "He was?"

"Yeah." Katrina looks serious, so there's no way to doubt her words. "So I think you're probably doing a good job in getting along with him. Maybe he's one of those guys who has trouble warming up."

Her calm words have transformed my entire attitude, my entire day. I'm suddenly excited. I want to get back to the office right away. "Maybe so. Thanks for telling me."

"Sure thing. Oh, hey, I broke up with my boyfriend a couple of weeks ago, so if you ever want to get together and do something, I'm game. I need to try to make more friends in town."

"I'd love to. Just give me a call anytime. But what happened with your boyfriend?" As long as I'd known her, she's had a serious boyfriend who lives and works in Charlotte, North Carolina. She went to visit him almost every weekend. I assumed they'd get married soon.

She shrugs. "It was long-distance. He found someone closer."

"Oh no! I'm so sorry."

"It's fine. I was..." She shakes her head. "Honestly, I wasn't all that excited about him anymore. I was just hanging on to... hang on. But now that I'm here every weekend, I'm finding I don't have many friends and don't have a lot to do."

"Well, I'm here, so call anytime. We can hang out."

"Thanks. I will."

"I better get back to my papers." I don't say it, but I mostly want to get back to Evan.

I can't believe he was saying nice things about me.

Does he really think my dissertation topic is brilliant?

I say bye to Katrina and leave the library, picking up my speed as I go.

4

Evan is still in the office when I arrive. Unlike me, he keeps fairly regular work hours, and he always stays at the office until at least five even if he doesn't have class or meetings. He probably doesn't like to work at home the way I do.

"Hey," I say as I come in, dropping my keys onto my desk and turning to face him.

He looks up from his computer. His expression is unsmiling but not angry. "Hi."

"I'm sorry about before. I'm not sure what got into me. I'm not usually so... irritable. I'm really sorry."

His mouth turns up just a little. His eyes soften palpably. "Evidently I'm an irritating kind of person, so that probably explains it."

"No, you're not!" I lower my tone as I continue. "You're really not that irritating. I should never have implied that about you. It's just that I'm usually really good at getting to know people, and I've been frustrated that I can't seem to get to know you."

He frowns. "You don't know me?"

"Of course not." My eyes are wide in surprise. "You think I've gotten to know you?"

"I thought we were making progress." He seems bothered by that piece of information, and he looks down at his desk as if he's thinking. "I'm afraid I'm never going to be the life of the party, if that's what you're hoping for."

"I know that. I mean, I don't care about that. I like all kinds of people. I just feel like you've got so many walls up I can't seem to get around them."

"Maybe if you wouldn't run away every time things start to get better between us."

Shit. He has no idea. I have to run away occasionally, but it's not because I don't want to get to know him.

It's because I want to tear his clothes off.

No way I can admit that to him.

I clear my throat and think fast. "I haven't run away that much. You just confuse me."

"What can I do to be less confusing?" Leave it to Evan to go about getting to know someone with the same sober determination he uses to tackle everything else.

"I don't know. Don't you ever just hang out and relax?"

"You want to hang out with me?"

Yes. Of course I do. In particular, I want to hang out in bed with him. "I just meant to get to know each other a little more. So we can get along better and be more comfortable sharing the office." There. That didn't sound too bad. That didn't give away my irrational lust for him.

He nods. "I like to bike, but that's obviously not your thing. I can go with you when you walk, if you'd like. Or..."

"Or what?"

"I was thinking about watching the Lord of the Rings movies since you like them so much."

My heart clenches. Ridiculously. "You were?"

"Yes."

"Maybe you can watch them with me. I would enjoy that."

"You would?"

"Yes. Would... would you?"

"Of course I would." His eyes never leave my face.

"What if you don't like them?"

"I'm sure if you like them, then they can't be that bad."

We smile at each other, and I let out a long breath.

I still have way too many papers to grade today, but things are definitely looking up.

ON SATURDAY NIGHT, Evan comes over to my house to watch *Fellowship of the Ring*.

I'm in a tizzy about it for no reason at all.

No. Reason.

But it feels like a first date.

Office Mate

I went to lunch and shopping with Katrina earlier today, and then I tried to do some reading for my upper-level class, and I got so bored that I fell asleep. I wake up two hours later with only fifteen minutes before Evan has arranged to come over.

Knowing him, he'll be exactly on time.

My little house is basically a square with two bedrooms and a bathroom between them on one side and the living room, dining room, and kitchen on the other side. The previous owner widened the doorways in the main rooms so you can see from the living room at the front of the house to the kitchen in the back.

Right now all three spaces are kind of messy because this was a paper-grading week and I haven't had time or energy to clean up. There are clothes and jewelry scattered around from when I've taken them on and off during the week and never gotten them back into the bedroom. There are books in piles in all three rooms. And there's a row of empty water bottles on the windowsill behind the couch.

I stand up, disoriented and trying not to panic.

I need to clean up before Evan gets over here. He's not going to want to hang out in a mess. His house is probably always perfectly clean with everything always in its place.

Mine is usually more like that than this. It's just that I had papers to grade this week.

I grab the water bottles and carry them into the kitchen to toss them into recycling, dropping three of them along the way. Then I flitter from room to room, collecting clothes and shoes and jewelry. The books I'll leave for last since they'll probably make him the least uncomfortable.

I glance in the mirror over my dresser after I dump my pile of clothes into the closet and shut the door. I'm a mess. My hair is loose and tangled around my face. My V-neck top is askew, showing a lot of cleavage and one of my pink bra straps. One of my cheeks is redder than the other from sleeping on it. And my mascara has smudged.

I whimper at the sight and run to the bathroom to restore my appearance since that has now become the priority in the minutes I have left. I brush out my long hair, debating about what to do with it. I'm still thinking as I wash my face and daub on a little makeup. I don't have time for a lot, and I don't want to look like I've primped too much for him.

I have no idea what I should wear. Maybe I should just keep on the thick leggings and long top I've been wearing all day.

But I want to look pretty.

I know it's not a date, but I still want to look pretty.

I launch myself into my big, stuffed closet and sort through all the possibilities hanging there. I glance at one outfit after another, making little whining sounds as my panic intensifies as the minutes pass.

Finally I see a casual knit dress with a low scoop neck and a fun blue and pink polka-dot print. I've always loved it. I feel pretty in it. But it's not any dressier than a T-shirt. I yank off my clothes and pull on the dress, glancing in the mirror and pleased with my reflection. Definitely curvy. Pretty and kind of sexy but still low-key. He won't think I'm dressed up in this. I smooth down the flyaways in my hair and am pleased with the result.

Fortunately, I planned ahead for food for tonight. Since he's not coming over until eight, we're not doing dinner, but I figured it's only polite to have some snacks. So I bought some gourmet popcorn and chocolate bark from a local food shop and also picked up a plate of cut fruit in case he's too healthy to eat the yummy stuff.

I'm about to take the fruit out of the refrigerator when the doorbell rings. I run to get it, swinging the door open to reveal Evan on my front porch.

I'm really glad I put the dress on since he's wearing neat khakis and a golf shirt and looking just as tailored and pulled together as he always does.

I wouldn't want him to think I'm a slob.

He smiles, his eyes running up and down my body. Something in his expression changes, and I look down quickly to check myself.

I look fine. Nothing out of place.

I check his expression again and see his eyes lingering on my cleavage.

I've got good cleavage. It's one of my best features.

Maybe—maybe—he's actually appreciating it.

I flush with pleasure as I let him in. I try to think of something to say, but words are escaping me at the moment.

He's been holding something behind his back, and he pulls it out as he enters. It's a bottle of wine.

I smile like a dope. "Oh goody!"

Yes, that's what I say. *Oh goody*. Never have I claimed I'm the most sophisticated of companions.

He chuckles. It's a real laugh. The kind I've only heard from him once. "I don't actually know if you drink or not, but I figured I'd take the risk."

"I do. Wine at least. I don't like beer, and mixed drinks go to my head too quickly. But I love wine."

"Good." He's glancing around my house, taking in the dark red couch, the fun prints on the side chairs, the lace curtains, and collection of throw pillows, area rugs, and collectibles. "This place looks like you."

"Is that supposed to be a compliment or not?"

"It is." He looks surprised. "I like it. It's really... nice."

"All right then. Come on in, and I'll open the wine before we start the movie. I've got snacks for us since who watches movies without snacks?" I pause. "Or maybe you do."

"I don't actually watch movies much at all, but snacks sound good to me."

I'm feeling more comfortable now. He doesn't seem as uptight as normal, and he's smiled and laughed like a normal person.

I really like how he looks. I want to run my hand over his closely cropped hair to see how it feels against my skin. He's always clean-shaven, but I want to rub my cheek against his jaw to see if he has any bristles. I want to untuck his shirt and get my hands beneath it so I can feel his lean abs, his straight back.

I catch myself before I go too far with that series of thoughts.

We're here so we can get along better as office mates.

We're not here for a sex marathon, no matter how tempting I find him.

He follows me into the kitchen as I open and pour the wine, and then we carry our glasses and the snacks I prepared into the living room. He sits on the couch beside me. Maybe just so we can share the popcorn.

I turn on a streaming service and pull up *Fellowship of the Ring*.

"Three and a half hours?" he asks.

"Oh. Well. It is long. And this is the extended version with extra scenes. We don't have to watch the whole thing if it's too long for you. I know you get up early."

"I'm sure I can manage." His mouth twitches up, and his eyes rest on my face. "I'm capable of staying up late, you know."

"Are you?" I can't believe I'm teasing him, but I am. "I thought maybe you were always in bed by nine so you could get up every morning at five."

"I don't go to bed at nine." He's obviously trying not to laugh, to keep his expression sober. "It's more like nine thirty."

I giggle as I press Play. I'm about to reach out to touch

him—do something silly like stroke his face or his chest—and I catch myself in time and cover by reaching for the popcorn instead.

He doesn't seem to notice.

Hopefully.

I forgot to put shoes on earlier, but I wouldn't have kept them on anyway. I get comfortable on the couch, stretching out and putting my legs up on my coffee table. My toenails are bright pink this week. After a while, Evan toes his own shoes off and does the same.

I try not to get uptight about whether or not he's enjoying it, but I do look over at him fairly often. He seems to be responding fairly well. He smiles at the funny parts and looks serious at the suspenseful parts, and occasionally when the movie events diverge significantly from the book, he frowns and pulls his brows together like he's thinking.

He definitely doesn't like that it's Arwen facing down the Black Riders instead of Frodo alone. But that's okay. I don't like that alteration either. Overall he seems to be getting into the movie as much as a man as reserved as he is can convey.

I enjoy the movie. I always do. And I like that it feels like I'm sharing it with him. It makes it more special somehow.

When the final credits start to roll, I turn to him.

His head is leaning back against the cushion of my couch, and he turns it toward me. His eyes are softer than

I've ever seen them, and there's a smile and something more in the dark depths. "Aren't you going to ask me what I think?"

"I figured you'd volunteer your opinion. You're the one who assumed it was just elves doing backflips."

"Well, there was some of that."

"He never did a backflip!" I pause, trying not to giggle. Then I add. "In this movie."

Evan laughs for real. The sound of it rolls over me, making me warm, making me safe, making me shiver. "It was good," he says. "I didn't like some of the choices, but that's inevitable in a movie version of a book. It was good. I'm glad I watched it."

"You are?"

"Yes."

"You're not just saying that?"

"Why would I just say that?" He's leaned a little closer to me. I can feel the heat from his body.

"To be polite."

His forehead wrinkles. "I never do things to be polite."

I gasp in outrage. "You're always polite!"

"I mean I never do things *just* to be polite. If I'm nice to someone, I want to be. If I say something, I mean it."

"Really?" I don't know why I'm whispering but I am.

"Yes, really."

"Because you've always been very polite to me. I thought you were just putting it on."

I've got one of my hands on the couch between us, and

he reaches over and covers it with one of his own. His clasp is warm, strong. I love how it feels. "I never put it on. I was nice to you because I... meant it."

I'm not sure why he stumbles over the words, but the slight hesitation makes my heart jump. I'm flushed and breathing too heavily, and an ache has grown in my chest and between my legs.

I try but I can't stop myself. The urge is simply too strong.

I lean over toward him until my face is just an inch away from his. Something flickers in his eyes. Maybe heat. Maybe a question. His lips part, and I close the gap between us.

The first touch of his mouth sends a surge of deep pleasure and excitement through me. My hands move up of their own accord to curve around his head. His hair feels just as delicious as I knew it would. It brushes against my palms with little tingles of sensation.

His mouth is moving with mine. He's definitely responding. But his hands are still in his lap. My tongue darts out to slide against the line of his lips, and he makes a low sound in his throat that's the most erotic thing I've heard in my life.

I whimper against his lips and lean closer.

He pulls back with a strange jerk of his body, breaking our mouths apart.

We stare at each other for a long moment, both of us flushed and gasping.

Then I realize what happened. I kissed him. I *kissed* him. And he pulled away.

"I'm sorry," I say, so embarrassed I can barely process it. "I'm really sorry. I didn't mean to make things awkward. I shouldn't have done that. I just... I didn't mean to."

I don't want to hear what he has to say. I don't want to see pity or discomfort in his eyes. I grab the popcorn bowl and the half-empty fruit plate and hurry into the kitchen, mostly to get away for a few minutes and recover my dignity.

I'm putting the leftover fruit into an airtight container when I'm aware that Evan has followed me. He comes up behind me at the sink, and I'm too afraid to turn around to look at him.

"Beck," he murmurs.

"I said I was sorry."

"Turn around."

I'm surprised by the authority in his voice, but I respond to it immediately. I'm not in a fit state to do otherwise. I turn around and gasp when I see he's only inches away from me. All I'm aware of is his strong, warm body. Trapping me against the sink. "What are you doing?" I ask when he takes a step even closer. His chest brushes against my breasts, making my nipples tighten excitedly.

"Checking something," he says, his eyes searching my face before he makes his move.

He kisses me.

This time it's definitely him.

I respond immediately, of course. How can I not, when this is exactly what I want to be doing? My arms wrap around his neck as he steps me back against the edge of the sink, the line of his body melding into mine. He explores my lips for a minute, his tongue and mouth surprisingly skillful and hungry. Then his tongue nudges insistently until I open for him, and he's all the way in my mouth.

I moan helplessly at the pure pleasure of it. His tongue sliding against mine. His hard body against my softness. I'm almost dizzy with how good it feels, and it's likely I would have fallen had I not been trapped between his body and the sink.

One of his hands is tangled in my hair, and the other has started moving over my body. It slides down my arm, tingling the bare skin there. Then he moves to stroke me over my dress, feeling down my side, running over the full flesh of my breasts, belly, and hips beneath the fabric.

I'm moaning again when he reaches my thigh. I'm not even embarrassed about it. There's no way I can stop the passionate sound even though it's mostly muffled by his urgent mouth.

Then I become aware of something else. He's getting hard. Aroused. I feel him against my middle. He's hard in his pants, and I shamelessly rub myself against it.

He huffs and breaks the kiss, panting against my skin. "Damn. Oh damn, Beck."

I grab for his head again. "Why did you stop?"

"Because I'm about to do more than kiss you."

"But that's what I want." I pull myself together to look him in the eyes. "That's what I want, Evan. Don't you want it too?"

I know he wants it physically. I can feel how much. But sex is so much more than physicality, and I've never pretended to believe otherwise. I want him to want this with more than his body.

"Fuck, do I want this," he mutters, his eyes blazing hot.

"Did you just say fuck?"

"Yes, why?"

"I've never heard you say that before."

"Do you want me to say it again?" He's leaning toward me again.

"Yes, please." I'm smiling up at him because he's relaxed again, and I'm hoping that means he wants this as much as I do.

He whispers against my lips. "Fuck." Then he kisses me again.

This time he's not holding anything back. His tongue is hungry and seeking, and his hands move all over my body, bunching up my skirt so he can stroke the bare skin of my thighs. I don't think my thighs are the most attractive part of my body, but he seems to like how they feel. He doesn't pull his hands away, and his fingers get more and more presumptuous.

"Can I touch you?" he murmurs, breaking the kiss just long enough to ask the question and let me answer.

"Yes. Yes, please. Touch me. Right now."

He chuckles into another kiss, and he adjusts his position so he can get his hand where he wants it. He rubs me over my panties. They're damp, so he's going to know how into this I am. How much I want him.

"Oh fuck," I hear him mutter as he tucks his fingers inside my underwear.

I gasp and make an embarrassing mewling sound when he finds my clit and starts to rub it. I manage to hook one leg around his legs to give him better access, and I move against his hand as best I can.

I can't focus on the kiss any longer since pleasure is building into a tight coil at my center. My head falls backward, and I let out a lingering groan.

"That's right, Beck," he murmurs thickly. "Come for me. I can tell you're going to come."

"Uh-huh. Uh-huh." That's actually what I say. I repeat it in helpless huffs of sound as I get closer.

His finger moves faster and harder against my sensitized clit until the tension finally breaks.

I cry out loudly, shaking through the spasms of release. I've always been loud in bed, and nothing in my experience has been as hot as this. Him rubbing me off against the kitchen sink in our clothes.

He strokes me through the orgasm until I finally relax against him. I'm limp and happy. I'm smiling like a fool.

He laughs and kisses me gently. "That was pretty damn hot."

"Was it?"

"Oh yes."

I reach between our bodies so I can massage him through his pants. He bites back a moan. "How does that feel?" I ask.

"That feels like I'm not going to last very long." He straightens up and opens his eyes, which had fallen closed with pleasure. "We can just stick with hands if you want. I don't know how far you want to go tonight, and I want you to know I'm okay with anything."

I almost melt with a wave of appreciation. I cup his cheek with one hand. It's just a little bristly. "I want to do everything, but only if you want it too."

"Everything? Because there's a world of sexual activities out there, and I'm honestly not sure if I'm up for everything right now. I mean, I can read up on it and do some research, and I'm sure eventually I can—"

I break into his words with a laugh. "I didn't mean—" I cut myself off when I see his face. I gasp. "You're teasing me!"

"Just a little." He tilts his head down to kiss my mouth gently. "We can have intercourse, if that's what you want."

"That's what I want."

He wraps his arms around me in what's almost a hug. "Me too," he murmurs against my ear.

He holds me like that for longer than I expect. I love it. The strength of his body. The way he's relaxing against all my curves as if he likes the feel of them.

Of me.

Then he moans and pulls away. "Bedroom?"

I nod. "Bedroom."

I lead him there. It's not exactly in its neatest state after my rush to get dressed, but I don't even care at the moment. I drag him over to my bed, yank down the covers, and then pull him down on top of me. Neither of us are wearing our shoes, so nothing but our clothes get in the way. And those don't last very long.

I'm so eager I'm already undoing his pants and pushing them down as we settle onto the bed. He raises himself up enough to shuck them off and also get rid of his socks and his shirt. I leer at his mostly naked body until he starts pulling up my dress. I help him get it off, and I have a moment of self-consciousness as he stares down at me in my bra and panties.

There's no way, at my size, I can wear lacy little bras. They'd never give me enough support. So my bra is more practical than anything else, although it's a pretty pale pink. I really don't want him to be disappointed in how I look.

He stares for a long time, and I can't see his eyes to check his expression. His breathing is accelerating though. I can hear it now.

Finally I can't stand it anymore. "Well?"

He raises his eyes, and I gasp at the heat I see in them. "I can't believe I get to see you out of your clothes. What did I ever do to deserve this?"

I giggle stupidly—in pleasure and relief. Then I lift up enough to unhook my bra in the back. "You're letting me see you without your clothes too, so I think we're even."

"Even?" He shakes his head, his eyes moving back down to my breasts as I pull my bra away. "I don't think so. My body is purely practical. Your body..." He reaches out to stroke one of my nipples with the pad of his thumb. "Your body is made for touching."

I don't know what's doing it for me more. His words or his gentle touch. But I'm limp with pleasure as I drop my bra over the side of the bed. "Your body is pretty good for touching too."

"If you say so." He's smiling when he kisses my mouth and then starts kissing his way down my throat. I arch my neck to give him better access, and then I arch my back as he reaches my breasts. He fondles one breast with his fingers as he suckles the other with his mouth. It feels so good—like so much all at once—that I moan and whimper and grow louder as he keeps it up. Soon I can't lie still. I'm squirming beneath him and clawing at his bare back.

"I've already come once," I gasp at last, when it feels like I'm going to explode from wanting him so much. "I'm good on foreplay."

He lifts his head. "Maybe I want you to come again."

"And you think I don't want that?" I shamelessly splay my legs apart. "Oh God, please. I'm dying here. I need to come so bad."

"Then let me do this for you."

"But you're so slow!"

He laughs softly, giving one breast a quick flick with his tongue before dragging his tongue down toward my belly button. "Are you always so impatient?"

"When I'm dying from needing to come, I am. Don't you need to come?"

"Desperately. It feels like I've been hard for you for weeks now. But I'm going to make sure to take care of you first."

If I wasn't a goner before, I definitely am now. I try to dampen my emotional response to him as he slides off my panties and pries my legs apart. He stares down at my groin the way he did my breasts earlier, and this time I see the possessive heat in his eyes.

He likes how I look. He really does. There's no way he can possibly be faking this.

He lowers his face and nuzzles between my legs. I make a silly sound in response.

He smiles and holds me open with his fingers so he can tease my clit with his tongue.

I clutch at the sheet frantically and moan.

"You're so responsive," he says, bending up my legs and raising my hips slightly so he can better reach me. I let him move me however he wants. "Do you have any idea how hot that is? You love the way I'm touching you."

"Yeah. Yeah, I do. Please, please, do it some more."

He chuckles, and I can feel it against my arousal. Then

his tongue is moving again. Sliding up and down and then playing at my entrance. I'm so wet I can feel moisture leaking out. He makes a murmuring sound of approval.

"Do you want me to use my hand or just my mouth?" he asks, nudging at my clit again.

"Your hand. I want to feel you inside me." I'm completely naked. Completely on display for him. And I'm not the slightest bit self-conscious about it since he seems to be enjoying this so much.

But not as much as I am. I'm having to fight not to squirm.

He slides one finger inside me, rubbing at my inner walls until I make a sobbing sound. Then he pulls it out and adds another finger. Pumps them exactly right.

I clamp down all around him, rocking my hips against the penetration.

"That's right. That's so good. You're so hot. So good. I want you to take what you want." His voice is the sexiest thing in all of creation. I swear it is.

"I want... I want... I want this." I arch up desperately, still clutching at the bedding beneath me. My hips are moving like crazy against his hand. He uses his other hand to hold me still enough to get his mouth down to my clit.

He sucks on it hard, and I come apart completely. I make loud, frantic sounds as I thrash with the intensity of the release.

He strokes me through the spasms. They last a long time, and he extends them with pressure on my clit.

I'm red and damp with sweat and completely boneless with satisfaction when he finally straightens up.

"There," he says with a little smile. His eyes are raking up and down my sprawled body as if he likes what he sees. "That's what I wanted to do first."

"Oh God," I gasp. "Oh God. I think I just died and went to heaven and then got sent back to do it again."

He laughs as I pull him down into an embrace, more a hug than anything sexual. "That sounds good to me."

"Now I want you to enjoy yourself too."

"You think I didn't enjoy what we just did?"

"I hope you did, but I want you to come now. I can go down on you if you want, or we can..."

"I believe intercourse was on the table." He lifts up enough to stroke his hands up and down over my body, lingering over all my fleshiest spots. "If you're ready."

"I'm definitely ready." I reach down to grab the waistband of his underwear, and then I pull it down over his hips and legs. My eyes are focused on his very firm erection, bouncing slightly from the motion. I make a throaty sound of approval at the sight of him.

"Is that good?" he asks, sounding genuinely curious.

"Definitely good." I smile at him as I reach into the drawer of my nightstand to grab a condom packet I keep there. "I assume you didn't bring any with you, so I've got one."

"Thanks. Good thinking." He rips it open and rolls it

on. Then he positions himself on his knees between my legs.

I stare at him in excitement, waiting to see what he'll do. "How do you want me?"

"How do you like it?"

"I like different positions. I come the easiest in doggie style."

Something flickers across his face. "Then you better turn over on your hands and knees."

My whole body tightens in response, and I do what he says.

He strokes my bottom for a minute, feeling the soft flesh, the line between my cheeks, and the rippled skin of my inner thighs. He parts my legs a little more and explores until he finds my wet entrance.

I hold myself up on my hands and knees and look back at him.

He's moving into position, but he meets my eyes for a moment. "Still want this?"

"Oh God yeah. Please. I want you to fuck me hard."

I never really considered myself someone to get into dirty talk, but it's really working for me tonight. With Evan.

He lines himself up and starts to edge into me.

I groan and arch my back as the penetration deepens.

"Okay," he asks, pausing midthrust.

"Oh yeah. Oh yeah. Better than okay."

"Me too. You feel better than anything." He pulls out

and pushes in again, this time making it all the way inside me.

He feels big and thick and solid inside me. I feel every inch of him. I make more helpless sounds as he shifts slightly and my muscles relax around him.

"How is it? Good?"

I really like how careful he is. How he's not just using my body as a way to get himself off. "It's amazing." I wriggle my butt. "I want you to move."

He starts to thrust, building up a fast, steady rhythm that's not particularly hard. It feels good. Really good. My body rocks with the force of his, my breasts and thighs and belly all jiggling deliciously. I huff out a loud sound with every thrust and don't care if I sound shameless.

After a few minutes, he starts to grunt too. His speed accelerates and so does the force of his motion.

"Yeah! Hard. I like it hard like that." I urge him on as the pleasure begins to coil again inside me.

He fucks me harder, grunting now like an animal. I look over my shoulder so I can see his face, and it's tense and damp and twisted in effort and pleasure. So incredibly hot. Almost primal. "Like this?"

"Yeah. Just like that. Hard. I need it hard."

He gives me what I need, so hard we're shaking the bed and bumping the headboard against the wall. The rhythmic sound of it turns me on even more.

My elbows buckle, and I bury my face in a pillow, sobbing as an orgasm starts to crest.

"That's right. You're going to come so hard. I can feel you, baby. Let it go. Let it go."

His voice is oddly soothing. It makes me feel safe enough to let go completely. The pleasure breaks, and I turn my head to gasp and then cry out loudly.

He keeps fucking me, and I keep coming, sobbing as the pleasure wracks my body. Then finally he reaches forward, hold of the headboard to brace himself, and grabs a fistful of my ass cheek with his other hand. He rolls his hips and jerks against my bottom, letting out a long, primitive sound of pleasure and dominance. Then he's coming too with hard jerks and loud huffs of sound.

He falls down beside me afterward, holding on to the condom so he doesn't lose it. We pant together, trying to recover ourselves.

I've had good sex before. Plenty of good sex.

But it's never been like that.

I wonder if he feels the same way.

I turn my head to look at him, and he smiles.

I smile back.

He definitely enjoyed himself. I'm not going to regret anything.

I've been wanting to do that with him for a long time.

5

It's a few minutes before we find the energy to get up.

Evan moves first, hauling himself to a sitting position with a soft groan and then lifting himself to his feet from there. He pads into the one bathroom in my little house, barefoot and naked. I hear the toilet flush. I hear the water running in the sink. Then he appears and leans down to grab his underwear from the floor and pull them on.

I watch him. I still love the sight of his body. It's strong and graceful both. Not bulky. There's no spare flesh or excess muscle anywhere. He said earlier that his body was purely practical, and he was partly right. He's aesthetically pleasing—very much so—but his body also looks made for use.

He doesn't do any sort of extra grooming—other than keeping his hair short and shaving his face every day. He's got dark hair on his chest, arms, and legs. And his groin. My eyes linger there as he pulls up his underwear.

He smiles at me—that little smile that seems to be his most natural expression. "You're staring."

"Admiring your body."

"If you'd drop the sheet, I could admire your body too." He grabs his pants and pulls them on.

I've pulled the covers up to my shoulder. After sex is over, I don't like to lie around naked. "Then I'd be cold."

He gives a huff of amusement as he pulls on his golf shirt. "I guess we couldn't have that even if it would give me something good to look at." He's dressed except for his shoes when he steps over to the side of the bed, leans down, and kisses me full on the mouth. "Thank you."

I was thinking about grabbing his head and deepening the kiss, but his words bring me to a sudden stop. *Thank you*? He's telling me *thank you*? "Um, you're welcome."

He straightens up, his smile fading slightly as he studies my face. "I had a really good time."

That's a little better. "So did I."

"Good. I'm glad." He hesitates, like he's thinking about saying something more or kissing me again. But he doesn't. He gives a weird little nod instead. "It's late. I better get going."

"Okay." Is he planning to call me? Does he want to do this again? Can't he give me some sort of clue? "I'll see you Monday then?"

"Yes." He does another of those stiff nods. "Monday. Thanks again."

Thanks again.

I'm sitting on my bed with a sheet still pulled up over my naked body as he leaves the room, leaves the house. I hear the front door open and close.

I process what just happened, and my eyes get bigger and bigger. My shoulders get tenser and tenser. My stomach clenches into a knot.

What the hell?

Thanks again.

I grab a sleep shirt from my dresser and yank it on as I hurry out into my living room to grab my phone. I pull up my text history with Jennifer and type out a new message.

I had sex with him, and he said thank you. Thank you!!!

It's a minute before she responds. *WHAT!*

All he said afterward was thank you, and then he left!

You had sex with him?

Yes and it was good, but then he said thank you and left!!!

Oh. Oh my.

I KNOW!

Jennifer is responding. I see the dots on the screen. But I can't wait. I add, *This can't be good.*

I don't know. Don't jump to conclusions. Do you want me to ask Marcus?

No! Then I change my mind. *Yes.*

I wait for a minute until she texts again. *He doesn't*

know. He said, well he's polite. Could mean anything. See how he acts on Monday.

I snarl at the phone. *That's a lot of help.*

Sorry. I wish I could interpret guy speak better.

I'm usually better at it myself, but Evan has me all upended. I groan out loud in my living room and tap out, *No. It's fine. Thanks for your help. I'll wait and see what happens.*

I hate waiting.

I hate not knowing.

I hate wondering if a guy likes me as much as I like him.

But I have that same knot in my gut that warns me that a guy who really likes me would make it clearer.

I really feel like I've been blown off.

I'VE DEFINITELY BEEN BLOWN off.

I know it for sure on Monday morning.

I've spent Sunday trying to talk myself down from jumping to conclusions, but he doesn't call, and as the time passes, that deep sense of foreboding intensifies.

This isn't good.

This can't be good.

I'm not inexperienced with men. I've dated a lot. I've signed up with every decent dating app that covers this area. I usually know immediately when a date is promising and when it's a flop.

But I'm completely clueless with Evan. Maybe because I had such a good time with him. I want him to feel the same way, so maybe I'm reading hope where there isn't any.

Any hope I have dies an instant death when I come into the office on Monday morning. I get there at seven thirty because I'm so jittery about seeing Evan again.

He smiles and says good morning. He asks me if I had a good Sunday. He comments on my getting to the office earlier than normal today.

And then he turns back to his computer to work on his lesson plans.

I sit down heavily in my desk chair. It rolls slightly, and I have to stabilize it. I look at Evan's back—the line of his shoulders, his straight back, the way his suit jacket fits him perfectly.

He's blowing me off. He has to be.

He doesn't want to have sex with me again.

It hurts. It can't help but hurt even though I lectured myself about being reasonable.

I feel rejected in an incredibly personal way. Being dropped after sex always feels that way. Sex is deeply personal whether people want to acknowledge it or not. But this feels worse. Because it feels like I shared more than my body with Evan.

I gave him something of myself on Saturday night, and he doesn't want it.

My throat hurts, so I swallow over it. I fight to keep my eyes from growing blurry. I've always been an emotional person, and it's hard to hide it now.

But I have to. I can't let him know he hurt me. We'd never be able to make it through the semester, the rest of the school year. We have to share an office, and we have to get along well enough to work in the same space.

So I have to be a mature person here and not make a big deal about it.

It feels like a big deal. It feels terrible.

But I'm a grown-up. And being a grown-up means accepting that the world isn't always what we think it should be. People aren't always what we want them to be.

This is a blow, but I'll get over it.

This is definitely why people advise against getting involved with people you work with.

This is terrible.

I turn on my computer and review my notes for class. Twenty minutes later, I leave the office with nothing more than, "I'll see you later."

At least class will hold my attention and I can forget about Evan for a little while.

"I can't believe he just said thank you," I say in what can only be described as a soft wail. "Thank you!"

Jennifer smiles sympathetically. When my ten-o'clock class was over, I'd stopped by her office instead of going back to mine, hoping she'd have a few minutes to talk. "And he didn't say or do anything this morning?"

"Just normal small talk. It was like the sex never happened. I mean really. Am I an escort or something, providing him a service that he thanks me for?"

"Now come on. He didn't treat you like that, did he?"

I settle my emotions enough to be honest. "No. He didn't. He did say he had a good time. But leaving with a thank-you after sex is a pretty crappy thing to do. I understand he doesn't want to keep seeing me. But how hard would it be to say he had a good time but he doesn't think it's a good idea to keep doing it? I wouldn't be happy, but at least I would feel like I hadn't had a door slammed in my face. *Thank you*."

I've been standing up in front of her desk, but she gets up and grabs her purse. "Let's take an early lunch. This is more than a quick office conversation."

I'm grateful for the gesture and glad for more delay before returning to my office.

As we leave the administration building and start walking toward the dining hall in the student center, Jennifer says, "Remember how things were with me after Marcus and I had sex the first time?"

"Yes, I remember. You were a wreck because he wasn't

making another move. But it's not the same thing. He told you he'd be happy to do it again if you wanted. If Evan said that, I'd be just fine. He didn't say that. He didn't say anything like that. What's wrong with the man?"

"I don't know. I really don't. Guys are hard to read."

"But they're not. They're usually not. Usually it's plenty clear if they're interested or if they're just along for the ride." I rub my face with my hands and admit, "I guess it's clear this time too. He doesn't even want to be along for the ride with me. Maybe I'm not good enough in bed for him."

"Oh my God, Beck. Don't be ridiculous."

"Fine. I am good in bed. At least I know the sex was good on Saturday night. But maybe he doesn't like the look of my body."

"Did he act like he liked the look of it?"

I force myself to remember clearly. Then I give a slow nod. "He seemed to."

"Then that's not it either. Don't start to tell yourself lies just because he's got you all in knots. You're beautiful. You're passionate. You're amazing in every way. If he doesn't want things to continue with you, it's not because you're not good enough."

I give her a wobbly smile. "Yeah. Thank you. I know you're right. I just feel..." I make a wordless burst of sound.

"I know that feeling well."

"I know you do. I think all women do. But I think I need to start being reasonable and admitting that he just doesn't like me enough."

We've reached the building and are opening the doors when someone comes up behind us. "Who doesn't like you enough?"

It's Katrina from the library. She's evidently heading to lunch too.

I give her a resigned smile. "A guy I slept with who hasn't said anything to me since."

"Oh shit," Katrina says, making a face. "I'm sorry."

I give Jennifer a significant look. "See? She agrees with me. It's a bad sign."

"Maybe," Jennifer says. We're all stopping in the lobby before entering the dining hall. It's early, so it's not very crowded yet. "The thing is, you still don't know. So if it's bothering you this much, the best thing to do is to talk to him."

"I can't—"

"I know it feels like you can't. But I'm speaking as someone who made a complete mess of things because I was too afraid to confront them head-on. It would be different if he was someone who isn't in your everyday orbit. You could just forget about him and move on. But he is in your orbit. You're going to see him every day. I really think you need to get things settled—just for your own peace of mind."

Katrina whispers with a quick intake of breath, "Are we talking about Dr. Jones?"

I scrunch up my face as I nod sheepishly.

"Oh my God! You had sex with your office mate, and

now he won't call you back?" Katrina's blue eyes are very wide.

I make a little sobbing sound and cover my face dramatically. "How is this my life?"

Katrina and Jennifer are both sympathetic, but they laugh at my outburst.

It actually makes me feel a little better.

EVAN IS out of the office when I return from the dining hall. I have no idea where he is. He usually eats lunch at his desk.

Maybe he's just in a department meeting or in the bathroom.

I shrug it off and try to focus on rereading a chapter of a book I'm supposed to teach about at one o'clock.

Early American history feels very unimportant to me right now.

He doesn't show up before one, and I head off to teach my last class of the day. He's not in the office when I return. I sit for a few minutes and decide I'll work from home for the afternoon. I'm not getting anything done as it is.

I'm getting my stuff together when he finally shows up. He stops in the middle of the floor, glancing over at me as I stuff some books in my bag.

"You leaving?"

"Yeah. Going to get some reading done at home."

"Okay." He stands for a minute and I wait, thinking with a catch of my breath that he might be about to say something.

He doesn't. He sits back down at his computer and clears the screensaver to show a document he left open.

I stare at the back of his head, breathing heavily.

I stand up and hook my bag over her shoulder.

I'm going to get out of here. It's just too painful.

Then I remember what Jennifer said.

Maybe I should say something. Having it settled—whatever that means—has to be better than this.

I come out from behind my desk and stop near his. "Um."

I expect him to turn from his computer, but he doesn't. "Did you need something?"

Did I need something?

"I guess not," I mutter, unable to hide the resentment from my voice. "I'm sorry to bother you."

I'm leaving the office when I hear him say, "Beck, wait."

I don't wait. I'm so upset I could throttle him.

To my surprise, he follows me. He catches up to me in the hall. "Beck, wait a minute. Wait a minute. What's the matter?" His eyes are dark and urgent. They're searching my face.

"What's the *matter*?" I repeat in a harsh whisper. I'm about to let him have it when a couple of students walk by.

There's no way I can get into this here.

There's probably little sense in getting into it at all.

"Nothing's the matter. Nothing at all." I take an abrupt step away from him when it looks like he's reaching for my shoulder. "I'm going home."

When I get home, I cry. I can't help it. But I don't let myself mope for long. I take a shower and eat a couple of cookies, and then I pull out a book I need to reread for my upper-level class. I stretch out on my couch to read.

It's a struggle to focus, but I eventually do, and I'm almost halfway through the book when the doorbell rings.

I sit up abruptly, glancing at the clock. Five after five.

I have no idea who would be at my house at this time.

Nothing to do but go answer the door. I gasp audibly when I swing it open to reveal Evan.

He's standing on my front porch in his suit and a sober expression.

He looks at me gravely as I process my surprise.

"What are you doing here?" I finally ask. It sounds rude, and I don't mean it to sound that way. But those are the only words I can shape.

"Can I please come in?"

I hesitate. I'm on the edge here, and it won't take much for me to completely fall apart. I really don't want to cry in front of him because he doesn't want me.

But I take a deep breath and step aside to let him in.

When he's in the entryway and I've closed the door, I ask again, "What do you want, Evan?"

"You're upset and I want to know why."

He could have said any number of things and I would have been able to respond in a calm, reasonable manner.

But he said *that*.

I choke on my indignation and fist my hands at my sides. "You want to know why? You want to know *why*?"

His eyebrows lift at my outraged tone. "Yes. I want to know why."

"Screw you, Dr. Evan Jones!" I have no idea why I use the honorific in my angry retort, but it just comes out.

His eyebrows go even higher, and his lips part slightly. He's surprised. Definitely surprised.

I don't even care. I let him have it. "How can you possibly not know what's the matter with me right now? Do you not understand women at all? Maybe it's perfectly normal for you to fuck women and leave them with nothing more than a thank-you and then pretend it never happened at all. But it's not normal for me. It's not normal, and I don't like it!"

His face changes, and he takes a step toward me. "You mean you want to do it again?"

I make a choking sound. My throat closes up so much that for a moment I can't get a word out. Then I explode. "Yes, I want to do it again, you big... big jerk!"

Okay. Not the most biting of insults. I'm never very articulate when I'm emotional like this.

Something has transformed in his eyes. He's not cool and serious anymore. He gets even closer to me, and he reaches out to touch me, but I pull away, still angry.

"It's not very nice to treat a girl the way you treated me!"

"I'm sorry. I'm really sorry. I thought..." He turns his face away, his expression tightening dramatically before he controls it. "I didn't know what to think. I've never been in this situation before. I didn't know if it was just a onetime thing, and I didn't want to make things awkward if it was. So I kept telling myself to take my cue from you, and you acted like... I just assumed that's all you wanted."

I'm gaping at him. "Of course that's not all I wanted. How big an idiot can someone be? How was I supposed to know you wanted to do it again?"

"I figured it would be obvious. I mean, how could I not want to do it again. I've never had sex like that before. I've never experienced anything so... I figured you'd know I was totally gone on you." He pauses, his eyes still looking for something in my face. "Isn't it obvious?"

"No, it's not obvious! You're the most hard-to-read man I've ever met in my life! If you want something, you need to come out and say it."

"Okay. Okay." He swallows so hard I see it in his throat. "I want to have sex with you again."

"All right then. I want to have sex with you again too."

"You do?"

That horrible knot in my stomach has finally loosened into a flurry of butterflies. "Yes. I do."

"Good."

"Good."

"Good."

I clear my throat, having to stop myself from saying good again.

"So?" he says. He reaches up and I think he's going to take my face in his hand, but he just brushes a strand of loose hair back behind my ear. It's the sweetest little touch.

"So what?"

"So if you want to have sex again, and I want to have sex again, maybe we can go ahead and have sex again?"

I bite my bottom lip, my cheeks flushing. I'm trying hard to contain my excitement, but I'm not sure I'm doing a good job. "Right now?"

"Why not right now?"

"I don't know. It's just after five, and you're still in your suit and my hair is a mess, and neither of us have had a shower since morning. So I thought maybe you'd want to wait until later in the evening until—"

He breaks off my babbling by kissing me.

It's a really good kiss. Strong and hungry and just demanding enough. I open to his tongue and melt against him as I reach up to hold on to his head.

He steps me backward until we tumble onto the couch, barely pulling out of the embrace. That seems like a reasonable place to end up, so I adjust to get more stable, and he climbs on top of me. The kiss deepens even more until we're rocking together to the rhythm of his tongue in my mouth.

He's already hard. I can feel his arousal pushing into me.

He's so hard. Hard all over. Hard in all the ways I'm soft. I hold on tight and squirm beneath him as a pressure of desire builds between my legs.

It's not long until he's fumbling to take off my clothes. First my top. Then my bra. Then my skirt and my panties. So then I'm naked on the couch while he has on all his clothes, and for some reason it's ridiculously hot.

He kisses and caresses me all over. I come once against his hand while he's suckling my nipple, and then I come again from his mouth, my legs hooked over his shoulders and my body making all kinds of shameless gyrations as I sob out my pleasure.

Since he's still wearing his clothes, I make him go into my bedroom to grab a condom from the drawer of my nightstand. The blinds on my windows are all open. I'm not going to wander around my house naked at this time of day.

Evan limps back, flushed and sweating and visibly aroused.

I giggle at the sight of him and pull him back down on top of me. This time I work on his clothes, and it's not long before he's as naked as I am and we've rolled on the condom.

Then he pulls my legs apart and folds one of my legs up toward my shoulder.

As you can probably guess, I'm not the most limber of women. I definitely can't manage weird contortions of my body, even in the interest of hot sex. But this position is doable for me, and it feels raw and slightly raunchy and vulnerable. My whole body throbs as he gets himself into position at my entrance.

"How's this?" he asks thickly. His eyes are running up and down over my body with a delicious kind of possessive dominance.

Like what he's seeing is his.

"Perfect."

"You want it like this?"

"Oh God yeah. Please. Take me like this." Again, I don't usually talk this way in bed, and it makes the whole thing better. Wild and deep and real at the same time.

I groan as he pushes his way inside me. My inner walls cling to his erection, and both of us gasp as we adjust to the penetration.

Then he braces himself on the arm of the couch and starts to thrust. It's hard and fast and animalistic, and I'm making loud, helpless sounds from the very beginning, babbling out how I need more, need it harder, need it so much.

He gives me what I need, and his soft grunts get louder as the tightness on his face intensifies. I can see he's working himself up to climax, and I'm almost there too.

I cry out, digging my fingernails into his firm ass and trying to ride him from below.

He lets out a muffled bellow, jerking his head to the side and growing momentarily still.

I sob at the halting of stimulation. "Not yet. Not yet. I'm almost there."

He makes a roaring sound and starts pumping again, so forcefully it shakes the couch, shakes my body. His groin slaps against mine.

Then I'm coming. Hiding my face in the couch cushion so my screams won't be heard outside the house. The pleasure continues as Evan keeps pushing against my contractions. Then he's coming too, jerking and moaning through his release.

We end up as a boneless tangle of limbs and flesh on my couch.

It's a long time before I can catch my breath. Even longer before I can move. Evan gets up eventually to take care of the condom, go to the bathroom, and pull on his underwear.

But he doesn't leave this time. He sits down on the couch, repositioning me so my head is in his lap. He strokes my hair and face.

If I wasn't a puddle of sated sentiment before, I definitely am now. I grab a throw blanket to cover my nakedness and cuddle up against him.

"That was amazing," I say when I'm finally able to form words.

"Better than amazing." He smooths my hair back from my face and meets my eyes. "You're the sexiest thing I've ever experienced in my life."

I smile at him, rather sappy. "Same to you."

He leans down to kiss me. "I'm sorry I messed up after the first time. I'm not good at... at this."

"I'm not sure anyone is really good at this."

"But you want to keep having sex with me, right?"

"Uh, yeah. I'd really like that."

He smiles, warm and soft and serious. Just like him. "I'd really like that too."

6

FOR THE NEXT MONTH, EVAN AND I SHARE AN OFFICE DURING the days, and we have a lot of sex in the evenings.

Needless to say, it's a very good month.

I don't tell anyone at the school except Jennifer and Katrina, and Evan doesn't tell anyone at all. Jennifer probably tells Marcus about it, but he's not going to blab. It seems smarter to keep things private at the beginning until we see what happens to us.

Small colleges are like small towns. Sometimes even worse. And I really, really, really don't want my students to know that I'm sleeping with the new English professor.

On a Monday morning in early October, I wake up when Evan gets out of my bed. He doesn't usually spend the night on workdays since he keeps such early hours, but we've spent most of the weekend together—except when he drove to Richmond to eat lunch with his sister on Saturday—and he never made it home last night.

I kind of like that he slept beside me all night. I wouldn't mind if he does it more often.

When I mumble out a "Good morning," he turns from where he's sitting on the edge of the bed, pulling on his T-shirt.

"Hey," he says with his quiet expression. "I didn't mean to wake you up."

"It doesn't matter to me. I can always go back to sleep for an hour or two." It's just barely five. I have at least an hour and a half to stay in bed before I need to get dressed and head to campus. If I push it, I can sleep until seven and still make it in time for my eight-o'clock class.

He lets out a long breath and slumps his shoulders like he's tired.

I reach out to wrap my fingers around his forearm. "You can stay in bed with me for a little while longer."

"I should get to the gym."

"You could, but you don't have to. Don't you deserve a morning off?"

"I had the weekend off."

He took a two-hour bike ride on Saturday morning while I was sleeping in, but otherwise he hasn't worked out since Friday morning. "Well, you can take one more morning off if you're tired."

He shakes his head, his eyes soft on my face. "Are you trying to tempt me?"

"Yes. I am. Why do you have to drive yourself so hard? You're in great shape, and working out four mornings a week instead of five isn't going to change that."

"You think?"

"Yes. I think." I've got a clench in my heart because he seems to be genuinely wavering. I never imagined I could actually talk him out of skipping his morning workout. Then I think of something. I push down the covers and pull up the bottom of the tank top I slept in, flashing my boobs. "There. How's that for temptation?"

I'm teasing. It's perfectly clear. And he chuckles in response. But his eyes are drawn to the sight of my bare breasts, and they don't waver, even after I pull my top down.

He likes my breasts. A lot. I mean *a lot*. That much has been made clear to me over the past month. Sometimes he just gazes at them with an awed expression as if he can't believe he's gotten so lucky. It's enough to go to a girl's head.

"That's pretty good temptation," he murmurs. He climbs over his side of the bed toward me.

I'm surprised and delighted by his shift in mood, and I kiss him with exuberant abandon when he claims my lips and moves over me.

We kiss for a long time. I'm so wrapped up in him and filled with sappy pleasure that the possibility of morning breath never even occurs to me. After a while, he starts paying attention to the rest of my body. He's a very attentive lover. He's never once found his own release without making sure I've come first. I've never been with a man so thoughtful and generous in the bedroom. I keep wondering if he'll eventually drop the sensitive act, but I honestly don't think it's an act.

I think it's just *him*.

It takes him a while to relax and warm up, but once he does, he's very, *very* warm.

I come once from foreplay and am feeling so much, so deeply for him that I want to do something special. So I turn him over onto his back before he can bring me to climax again.

"What are you doing?" he asks, blinking up at me as I pull down his underwear. His smile is pleased, almost drowsy. "You want to be on top this time?"

"Something like that." I kiss my way down his chest and belly until I reach his groin. He's already hard, and I see his erection twitch as my mouth hovers over it.

I've gone down on him before, but he always stops me before he comes.

I want him to come this time.

I look up toward his face and meet his eyes for a moment. His are smoldering. Tense.

I lick a line up the underside of his shaft, and he lets out the sexiest sound. Something between a sigh and a growl.

It gives me all kinds of shivers.

I try to focus on the task at hand, however, so I play with his balls as I give the tip of his erection a firm suck.

His hips buck up. "Jesus, baby, you're going to kill me."

"What do you think I'm trying to do?" I suck him again.

He groans and tosses his head back and forth. It's intoxicating to see him so helpless, so out of control. "I'm serious. I'm not going to last long like this. So if you want to do something else…"

"This is exactly what I want to do." I wrap my fingers around the base of him and slide my mouth down until it meets my hand. I apply rhythmic suction as he rocks his pelvis in tight little pumps.

I can see he's getting closer. The muscles of his thighs and belly tighten. His fingers fumble against the sheet. He arches his neck and lets out a long groan as he gives a few helpless jerks into my mouth.

Then he's coming in shakes and spasms. He grabs for my head and holds it in place. His face transforms with a look of primitive satisfaction that gives me as much pleasure as another orgasm would have.

I awkwardly swallow his semen. It's not the nicest part of this activity, but he didn't actually come that much since we've already had sex so many times over the weekend.

He's limp and gasping as I crawl up his body and settle myself at his side. He wraps one arm around me and presses a few kisses into my hair. "Thank you, baby."

"You're welcome."

"You're good at that."

"I'm glad you think so."

"But you've blown your chance for another round," he says. "I'm not sure I can get it up again this morning soon enough to go again."

I giggle. "I've blown my chance."

He snorts, realizing his unintended wordplay. "Something like that."

I nuzzle his neck. "I already came once, and that's not counting all the other times I've come this weekend. You take very good care of me. I wanted to do that for you."

"Okay. Thank you."

"You're welcome again."

He is a very polite man, but I've gotten to know him better now. And I've discovered that he was telling me the truth when he said he only says nice things when he means them.

So he's genuinely grateful for the blow job, and that makes me very happy I made the effort.

We lie together enjoying the aftermath for a while. I feel a little tired but not like I'm going to go back to sleep.

I want to talk to him. I want to feel close to him.

And the only way to get what I want is to ask a question.

So I finally say out of the blue, "Why did you come to Milford?"

"What do you mean?"

"I mean why did you take the job at Milford? Didn't you want a bigger, more impressive school?"

"I don't know." He's idly stroking his fingertips up and down my arm. "What makes you think I could have gotten a job at a better school?"

"Don't be that way. Are you telling me you got no other job offers?"

"I got three," he admits.

"And were the other two at bigger universities where you could have had more time for research?"

"Yes."

"So why didn't you take them? You're going to have to teach a lot at Milford. You won't be able to do as much writing and research."

"I know."

He doesn't say anything more, and it bothers me. He hasn't answered my question, and I really want him to.

As I lie there and wait, it occurs to me that he's told me nothing about his background. Nothing very personal beyond his hobbies, his time in graduate school, and the places he's traveled. He's never talked about his family except mentioning his lunches with his younger sister. He's never told me about friends or past relationships. I've told him everything, and he's never told me much of anything.

Here I was thinking we were getting close, and we weren't. Not really.

When the silence drags on too long, I say softly, "Evan?"

He lets out a breath. "Yeah. I took the job at Milford because it was closest to my family."

"Really? Was it that important you be close to them?" I try to keep my tone casual, like I'm not making a big deal out of it.

But it feels like a big deal. He's finally telling me something.

"Not my folks. But my sister. I wanted to be close to her."

"Oh. Is everything okay with her?" I'm not exactly sure how to ask this question, but it seems like he has a particular reason for wanting to be close to her, and I want to know what it is.

"Yeah. She's good. Just seventeen. And... I don't know... lonely."

"She doesn't have a lot of friends?"

"No. She's a lot like me. She's really smart and loves reading and writing and would hide herself away in her room all the time if she could. She's doing fine. I don't think she's in any sort of trouble or anything. But I think she's lonely. She feels like she doesn't fit in—the way I did most of my life. And so I want to be there for her."

I think about what he's told me. How much more he's told me in the past minute than he's ever told me before. I reach over and rub his flat belly with my palm. "That's nice of you. To be a brother to her like that."

"I..." He trails off. Clears his throat. Then starts again. "I felt like I didn't really have anyone growing up. Not anyone like me. I don't want her to feel the same way."

"So you didn't feel close to your parents?"

He gives a half shrug as an answer.

"Evan?" I prompt.

"It's just that they're different. From me and from Sara. I don't want her to feel alone the way I always did."

It means something to me that he's opened up this much. I adjust closer to him so I can nuzzle his neck. I keep stroking his chest and belly.

We don't say anything for a long time. It feels like if I ask another question, I'll push too far and he'll close up again.

I'm right about that.

After several minutes, I say softly, "Thanks for telling me all that. Why don't you ever talk about your family?"

"There's not much to say." His mood has changed. He turns over onto his side with a smile that seems intentional rather than genuine. "My family isn't all that interesting. Not nearly as interesting as kissing you."

Before I can respond, he's kissing me again, and it's hard to say no to that. We kiss and he caresses my breasts, stomach, and thighs until I'm really turned on. He gets me off with his hand, and I gasp out my release against his mouth.

"Okay," he says when he finally pulls away. "We've had about all that we have time for this morning. I need to run home so I can get dressed and get to work on time."

"Yeah. I need to get up too. I have class at eight." I stretch under the covers, enjoying the lingering effects of my orgasm. "See you in the office."

He gives me a quick kiss before he leaves.

It's only after he's gone that I realize he very effectively changed the subject so he wouldn't have to keep talking about his family.

A FEW DAYS LATER, I stay on campus until five, putting together a conference paper proposal that's due today. I always leave things like that until the very last minute. But I get it submitted before the deadline, and since it's five, I wait a few minutes until Evan is ready to leave so I can walk home with him.

There aren't a lot of students meandering around at this time of day. Only a few classes meet at this time, and it's too early for most of the students to be heading for dinner. But the sidewalks are filled with the staff who work regular business hours heading for their cars to go home.

Several of them wave or greet us. I look carefully, but no one is peering at us with any real curiosity or suspicion.

Faculty walk around campus together all the time, and evidently it doesn't cross anyone's mind that something might be going on between Evan and me.

It's good. It's better that way. But it bothers me a little.

I'm having sex with Evan. We *are* together. Maybe not seriously, but in a real way. There's no reason why we can't be even more than that in the future.

I'd be a good match for Evan. People should be able to see it.

"What's the matter?" he asks as we cross the parking lot that's the shortest route to our neighborhood.

"Nothing."

"You look like something is annoying you." His eyes search my face. "Is it me?"

I giggle. "No. It's not you. You've been very unannoying today."

"Ah. That's good then."

I experience a definitely swoony feeling at the fond look in his eyes. I want him to look at me like that all the time. No sense in denying it.

I'm still trying to process the reality of this feeling when we reach the vacant lot. I watch as Evan steps into it. He leans over to pick up a bottle cap that must be today's gift from the crows and then tosses out some peanuts in shells he's had in one of his pockets.

I shake my head as he comes back to me. "You're giving the crows peanuts in the evenings too now?"

He shrugs and gives me a sheepish look. "They discovered that I walk by at this time every day and started waiting for me in the evenings too. I hate to disappoint them when they give me so many presents."

I laugh and reach over to take his arm companionably, mostly because I feel the need to touch him. "You've got a soft heart, you know. You should let more people know about it."

"Uh-huh," he says dryly.

"I mean it. Why do you hide it?"

He gives me another shrug. "I have an older brother. It wasn't smart to act too softhearted with him around."

I almost gasp at that revelation—almost the only thing he's ever said about his family other than the existence of his younger sister. "Was your brother hard on you?"

"Oh yeah. He was popular and good at sports and always told me I wasn't tough enough. He..." Evan clears his throat. "He constantly tried to toughen me up."

"Oh. He was mean to you then?"

"Sometimes. He was a brother. And I liked school and books and ideas and couldn't throw a ball to save my life."

I'm an only child, so I've never had a brother. But I don't like the sound of that answer. I also don't like the resigned look in his eyes, as if he's used to his brother not being good to him. So much so that he doesn't expect anything else. He told me he was always lonely as a child, and my heart breaks for that smart, isolated little boy. "Are you... are you close now?"

"No."

That tells me something I need to know. If his brother had grown up into a decent guy, Evan would make an effort to stay close to him. He'd taken the job in Milford so he could spend time with his sister. He'd do the same thing with his brother, unless there was some reason not to.

His brother isn't a good guy.

He isn't a friend to him.

He must have hurt Evan in the past.

He certainly taught Evan to hide anything that could be taken as weakness—including his very kind heart. That's probably why Evan is so reserved and uptight now. He's learned to hide his real self.

I don't like Evan's brother although I know almost nothing about him.

I don't like him at all.

"How much older is he than you?" I ask, trying to think of easy questions that won't prompt Evan to close up.

"Three years."

"And your sister is a lot younger than the two of you?"

"Yeah. She's just seventeen. Thirteen years younger than me. She was a surprise baby for my folks."

"Are you going out to see her this weekend?"

"For lunch on Saturday. I'll be back to hang out for dinner if you're available." He gives me another one of those hot, soft looks I love.

I smile at him like a dope. "I'm available."

I've put all my dating apps on hold. Even though Evan and I aren't serious yet, it would feel wrong to go out with anyone else. And the truth is I don't want to.

I don't want to be with anyone but him.

I wonder if he feels the same way.

I wonder if it's too soon to ask him about it.

THE FOLLOWING WEEK, we're both in the office on a Thursday afternoon. I've been grading papers from my upper-level class most of the day, but I've managed to finish them, so I'm on that post-grading high. I've got the worst of my work done for the week. Now I just have to make it through classes tomorrow, and I'll have another weekend with Evan.

At least that's what I'm hoping. He has lunch with his sister on Saturday, but I'm hoping he'll want to hang out with me for the rest of the time the way he did last weekend.

It might be nice if we were a surer thing. More than just a lot of sex.

Neither one of us has said anything yet, and that has felt fine to me because it was just at the beginning.

But it's been more than a month now. We get together every single day.

We're now beyond the beginning, and it might be nice to not have to wonder if he wants to spend the weekend with me.

It might also be nice for other people to know that we're together so it doesn't feel so much like a dirty secret.

Maybe I'll say something. Ask him about it.

Maybe.

It takes a lot of courage to do something like that when guys are so often skittish about commitment. I know in theory that if a guy is reluctant to commit, then it's probably best to just let him go.

But I don't want to let Evan go.

I want to keep him.

And I don't want to move too fast and pressure him unnecessarily.

It's just been a month.

That's not really very long.

It's almost four in the afternoon, and I'm finalizing my lesson plans for tomorrow before I go home when Jennifer taps on the open office door and comes in.

"Hey," I say with a smile, turning away from my computer. "What are you doing in these parts?"

"I needed to take a walk, and I wanted to know if you want to have dinner after work. Marcus has to work this evening, so we're having an early dinner in Milford before his meeting. I thought maybe you'd want to join us."

"Sure," I say. "That sounds great." I haven't hung out with Jennifer as much as I used to because she spends so much time with Marcus and they live forty-five minutes outside Milford. So I'm happy about the invitation.

Jennifer looks over at Evan. "You could come too if you want. It will just be me, Marcus, and Beck." It's clear to me why she adds that last sentence. To reassure him that the only people at the meal will be those who already know about my relationship with him.

Evan looks surprised but smiles. "Oh. Thanks. But I don't think so. I'll probably work late."

"Okay. No worries." Jennifer shoots me a quick look, and I give her a wordless twitch of a shrug in response.

But this bothers me too. That Evan doesn't want to hang out with my friends.

What kind of relationship does he think this is? Is it really just sex to him?

Jennifer doesn't linger on the topic, which is a relief. She shifts her eyes to the framed posters on the wall. Then she says with exaggerated sentiment, "Oh Aragorn! My first and best boyfriend."

I giggle. Even more when Evan turns back to the conversation with an arch of his eyebrows. "You don't really want Aragorn, do you?" I ask Jennifer.

Her mouth drops open. "Of course. Why wouldn't I?"

"Because he's kind of... I don't know... condescending."

"He is not. He's lofty, but he's king, so he's supposed to be. I do like him better as Strider, but still..." Jennifer looks over at Evan. "Beck can just never forgive him for rejecting Éowyn."

"I have heard something along those lines when we watched the movies," he says with a fond smile at me.

"Of course I don't forgive him! He obviously has no taste in women at all. But it's not just that. In the books I like him as Strider too, but he just gets too... too high at the end. Not human enough. And in the movies—well, in the movies he's just like every other jerk of a guy I've gone out with. Leading Éowyn on—you can't tell me all those soulful looks didn't mean something—and then acting all skittish when she takes him seriously and patting her on the head and pretending he never gave her the wrong idea. It's such a guy thing to do. Nope. Just don't like him."

Jennifer laughs, and Evan is smiling, but he's also watching me closely.

It makes me a little self-conscious, and that makes me fluttery, which means I don't guard my words as much as I should as the conversation continues.

Jennifer gives Evan a conspiratorial wink. "Beck has eyes for no one but Faramir."

"That's not true," I object. "When I was a teenager, I was all into Legolas, of course. And lately I've been thinking that, well, maybe Gandalf has something going for him."

That gets a laugh from both of them, as I intend.

"But you like Faramir the best?" Evan asks, his expression sobering.

"Yeah. Sure I do. Who wouldn't? Think of poor Éowyn, quite unfairly rejected even though she killed the freaking Witch-king of Angmar and saved the day. The man she wants doesn't want her. He wants some barely there elf chick instead. And here comes a really good guy who looks at her and sees everything he wants. He recognizes her for what she is. For all her worth and value and beauty. He sees it in her, and he wants nothing else. Of course he's the best guy. If you've got to choose one of them for a boyfriend, he's the one I'd choose."

"Sam would be pretty good too," Jennifer says, smiling although her eyes are deep as if she knows I'm in earnest.

"For sure. Sam would be a good boyfriend too. But no Aragorn for me, no matter how hot he looks with that sword."

I suddenly realize that Evan's in the room and he's heard everything I've said.

I meant it. Everything. But maybe it reveals too much about my feelings.

Maybe he thinks I'm talking about him somehow.

I cover my nerves with a teasing question. "What about you, Evan? Who would be your girlfriend? And if you say anyone except Éowyn, I'll forever doubt your judgment."

He laughs, his face relaxed although his eyes never leave my face. "Éowyn for sure. For one thing, she's the only woman in the books who feels fully human."

That is a good response. An Evan-like response. I feel better about my ramblings and decide he hasn't read anything into them he shouldn't.

Jennifer confirms dinner with me and then leaves the office.

"You'd be more than welcome at dinner with us," I say lightly after she's gone.

Evan glances over. "No. It's fine. No need to give people ammunition for gossip."

Okay then. That makes it clear.

He still doesn't want anyone to know about us, which means he's nowhere close to being serious about me.

Better to know it now before I'm too far gone to pull myself out.

7

For the next week, I dither around, trying to figure out what I should do.

Every time I'm on the verge of saying something to Evan, he acts particularly sweet and attentive, so I convince myself he really likes me after all and I'm unreasonable to expect too much too fast.

I've always been more decisive than this. I've always seen relationships clearly and known when to hope and when to pull out.

I'm not sure why Evan has gotten me all angsty. I should be able to approach this relationship the way I have all my other ones. Knowing what to do and not hesitating to do it.

But I don't want to lose him unless I have to, and I'm not yet sure that I have to.

So I get through the next week in a state of fluttery

emotion. Half the time I'm reveling at being with him, and half the time I'm terrified that he's just having fun with me.

We haven't even been together two months. It's too soon to press the issue with him.

Isn't it?

By the following Monday, I'm emotionally exhausted. I'm not going to make it much longer in this uncertain state, and the knowledge that a confrontation is coming makes me anxious.

Plus I have an enormous stack of essay exams to grade from my survey classes.

I feel grumpy all day. At three thirty, I'm sitting behind my desk trying to make some headway on grading, and I'm irrationally annoyed by Evan, who's been nothing but nice all day.

How dare he look so calm and handsome and smart and sexy and content when I feel like I'm falling apart?

It's just not right.

After a long stretch of silence, he pulls me out of the exam I'm trying to focus on by asking, "Are they really that bad?"

I blink and look over at him. "What?"

"The exams. Are they really that bad?"

"They're about normal. Why?"

"Because you seem like you're on the edge over there." His eyes are as observant as ever, taking in my messy hair (which keeps slipping out of the clip I pulled it up with this morning), my worn-off makeup, and the thin cardigan I keep taking off and putting on over my sleeveless top.

"I feel like I'm on the edge," I admit, rubbing my eyes and trying to hold back a wave of frustration.

His forehead furrows. "Is it just the grading?"

"I don't know." I slump back in my chair. "It's just..."

This is my moment. My chance to express how I've been feeling. He's asking. His eyes are searching and slightly concerned.

I can just tell him. I need a bit more clarity about our relationship. That's it.

Just say it.

I'm angry at myself even as I make the decision, but I simply can't do it.

Because if his answer isn't what I want it to be, then I'll have to break up with him. And I'm afraid that might break me.

"What's the matter, Beck?" he asks, his tone more sober than before.

I shake my head and rub at my scalp with my fingertips. "Just one of those days, I think. When everything makes you crazy. I guess you don't have days like that."

"I do occasionally."

"I've never seen you have one of those days."

"Maybe you don't see everything."

I drop my head on my hands. "Sometimes it feels like I don't see anything."

He doesn't answer, and my eyes are hidden by my

hands, so I don't know what he's doing until I hear the office door click. We always leave it open when both of us are in here, so this is significant.

I look up. "What are you doing?"

He comes over to my side of my desk. "Stand up."

I frown at him, more confused than annoyed. "What are you doing, Evan?"

"I said stand up."

I roll my eyes, but I don't have energy for an argument, so I do as he says. I stand up beside my desk chair and meet his eyes confrontationally. "You think bossing me around is going to make me feel better?"

"No. I don't." His voice is soft and husky. He pulls me into a hug. "I just wanted to do this, and I couldn't when you were sitting down."

It's the last thing I expect, and it completely does me in. I press myself against his familiar body and soft suit, and I shake.

His arms are tight, comforting, supportive. They're exactly what I need to feel.

His heart beats beneath my ear, fast and steady. He doesn't say anything.

He doesn't need to.

We hug for a long time until I'm soft and relaxed against him. Only then does he loosen his arms and draw back to look down into my face. "You okay?" he asks.

I nod, my face tightening briefly with emotion. "I'm good. Thanks."

He angles his head down to press a soft kiss against my lips. "Has anyone ever told you you're very kissable?"

I giggle. "Uh, no."

"And very huggable."

"No again."

"And very fuckable."

My giggles turn into uninhibited laughter. "Fuckable?"

"What's wrong with that?" His expression is a picture of confused innocence.

I know he's playing it up on purpose to make me laugh. "No one who looked at you would ever know you have a dirty mouth."

"Obviously looks can be deceiving." Then he pauses. "I don't have that dirty a mouth."

"No. You don't." I pull him down into another kiss and murmur over his lips. "Just dirty enough."

He slides his hands down until they're holding my bottom as our mouths move together. I'm not sure when the exact moment is when the embrace changes from sweet and fond to sexy, but it definitely does. It's not long before I'm rubbing myself against him and he's growing hard in his trousers.

A glimmer of reason cuts through my haze of lust, and I mumble, "Should we be doing this? We're in the office."

"I locked the door," he says, squeezing the soft flesh at the back of my thighs in a possessive way that thrills me. "We'll have to be quiet, but it's good with me if it's good with you."

I pause only briefly. Now that I have my hands all over him, I really don't want to let him go. I give him a slanting smile. "It's good with me if you think you can be quiet."

He chuckles and starts bunching up my skirt. "You're the one who likes to be loud."

I huff and help him by shimmying out of my panties. "You can be pretty loud too, you know."

"Then we'll both have to stifle our instincts." He grows still for a minute, looking from me to the desk behind me. "Why don't you bend over the desk, baby?"

My whole body clenches in excitement, and I do what he says.

He positions me the way he wants, parting my legs a bit and pushing my skirt up the rest of the way to bare my bottom.

"I've got a condom in the zipper pocket of my purse," I tell him.

I heard him in my purse, then the unzipping of his trousers and the rustling of fabric, and then the ripping of the condom packet. Then he's feeling between my legs to make sure I'm ready (I'm definitely ready) and lifting my hips enough to position himself.

I bite my lip over a moan as he enters me.

It's so raw and real. Bending over the edge of the desk in my own office, surrounded by my work furnishings. The hard edge of the desk pushes into my belly, and I reach out to hold on to the opposite end to stabilize myself. Evan is big and hard and intrusive inside me, and his thrusts are short and forceful.

We don't have time for a lot of foreplay or experimentation. This has got to be down and dirty by necessity.

We're both huffing, and I catch myself every time I get too loud. When his fucking starts to feel really good, I have to let go of the desk and stuff my fist in my mouth to smother the sound.

"Can you come, baby?" he asks after a few minutes, leaning farther over and talking thick and soft. "I'm not gonna make it long."

"Yeah. Yeah. Gonna come." The response is forced out in broken pants. My whole body is flushed and damp, and my hair is falling into my face, and my body is about to erupt.

He grabs hold of my ass cheeks and thrusts hard and fast.

I sob over my fist as the tension finally breaks, and he comes right after me with a series of stifled groans.

He holds the position for a minute afterward, stroking my bottom and thigh with one hand. Then he pulls out, takes care of the condom, and pulls up his trousers. He helps me stand up, and I push down my skirt before he pulls me into a warm embrace.

"You're amazing, baby," he murmurs against my neck. "Amazing."

My heart melts.

I've got nothing in the world to complain about.

It hasn't even been two months.

Things between Evan and I are going just fine.

OUR LOVEMAKING in the office sustains me for another two weeks, but slowly those flickers of anxiety start to show themselves again when he continues to tell me nothing more about his family and background, and he makes no move to bring our relationship out into the open.

There's no rational reason not to. Relationships between faculty in different departments are not against policy and are not problematic. We have no real professional conflicts to worry about.

There's absolutely no explanation for the hesitation except he doesn't want anyone to know he's having sex with me.

Secret relationships are only hot for a little while. Soon they become cumbersome and stifling. Not to be able to share your life with the people around you. Not being able to show the world whom you care about and want to spend time with.

Evan comes over on a Friday night, and we make dinner together and watch the last Hobbit movie. He's seen all six movies now, and we have a good time talking about the choices made for the film. It's almost midnight when I get into bed. Evan's taking a shower, so he hasn't joined me yet.

I feel mostly content. It's a good relationship. The things that bother me aren't all that big.

But they're bothering me more and more, and I know it's wrong that I still don't want to admit that to Evan.

Maybe a little part of me wonders if I deserve a guy like him and is afraid that if I try to stake a claim, he'll slip right out of my hands.

I don't like admitting to that kind of insecurity. I've grown so much over the past five years. I love myself and I love my body, and if other people don't appreciate me, then it's their problem, not mine.

But I guess I'm not totally there yet. And I catch myself wondering why Evan is with me and not with a prettier, slimmer, more polished and elegant woman.

Maybe that's why he doesn't want to make our relationship public. Maybe that's why he doesn't want me to know anything about his family.

Maybe it's me.

I lie in bed while the shower runs, and I mentally talk myself out of believing those lies. They might still be a part of me, but I don't have to welcome them into my mind, my soul.

By the time the shower turns off and Evan comes back into the room wearing nothing but a pair of sleep pants, I'm back in control of my worries and insecurities.

I smile at him as he comes to bed because he's clean and sexy and so incredibly smart. Because he's got a fond look in his eyes that I love.

He climbs under the covers beside me and pulls me against him, wrapping me in a soft embrace. "I had a good evening," he says, pressing little kisses into my hair and across my forehead.

We haven't even had sex yet, so his words definitely make me feel good. "So did I."

"I never used to have such good evenings."

I adjust so I can see his face. "Really? What were your evenings like?"

"Way too many of them were spent alone with my books."

"That's kind of sad."

"I know. I didn't realize it at the time, but I definitely do now. A lot of my life was spent being lonely."

My heart has started to race. It feels like he's opening up again. I want it to happen so much, but I also don't want to pounce on the opportunity and make him feel pressured. I ask lightly, "Did you have any friends?"

"Some casual friends from school, but no one I ever felt close to." He pauses. "Not until I was an adult, I think."

"Surely there was someone in your school who was like you. Who liked books and studying and things."

"Yeah. Yeah, there were. But people kind of fell into groups, and I never fell into any of them. It's probably my fault. I always held back."

"Why?"

"Because..." He clears his throat. "Because every time I

tried to get close to someone, I ended up getting rejected. So I learned not to try."

"Oh Evan." I give him a full-body hug. "That's just not right."

He hugs me back, and I can tell he's taking comfort in me. "It's not that big a deal. I was a kid. A lot of kids don't have an easy time of it. I made it through. I grew up. I got better."

"I know you did. But I still think your family could have looked out for you better, the way you're doing with Sara."

He shakes his head and sighs. "I've just never been close to my family." He clears his throat. "Speaking of..."

I hold my breath. Is he actually going to tell me more about his family?

"They're coming into town tomorrow. Just for the weekend."

"Oh really?" Again, I pitch my voice as easy and unconcerned.

"Yeah. Sara and my parents. So I'm going to need to spend time with them tomorrow afternoon and Sunday morning. I won't be able to hang out with you all weekend like we've been doing."

My fluttering heart drops like a rock. "Oh. Okay. That's no problem." I bite my lip, but I can't hold back the next thing. "I wouldn't mind meeting them, if it's not too weird or anything."

He's silent for a few moments. Too many moments.

Then he says, "It would be weird. I'd rather not get into all that."

My burgeoning hope dies a quick death. "Okay. No worries. I told Katrina we could get together tomorrow anyway. I'll just hang out with her."

"Sounds like a good plan."

And that's it. That's the conversation.

I don't have time to process it and decide how I feel about it before Evan's making his move. He rolls me over on my side and kisses me, deepening the kiss as I respond.

Of course I respond. I always respond to him. I want as much of him as I can get.

We have sex under the covers. He makes me come with his fingers inside me and his mouth on my breast, and then he moves on top of me and takes me in missionary position. I squeeze my hand down to my clit to rub myself off so I can come again while he's inside me.

He mutters out a lot of things I want to hear while he's working up to climax. About how beautiful I am. How passionate I am. How hot and sexy and amazing I am. How he wants me so much. How no one has ever made him feel as good as I do.

And I believe him. I want to believe him.

But I don't understand why, if all that is true, he won't share more of himself with me.

Because I'm finally having to acknowledge that—as incredible as he makes me feel—this relationship is no longer enough for me.

I don't want a hot fling or a guilty secret.

I want a man who wants to share my life and share his with me.

And maybe Evan doesn't want to do that right now.

Maybe he never will.

THE NEXT DAY, I get together with Katrina for lunch, and we have plans to see a movie afterward.

We talk about how she's finally over her breakup and how she'd like to start dating again and actually have a little fun.

Then she asks me about Evan.

I tell her the truth. The whole truth. I've got to talk to someone, and Jennifer has been busy this week with Marcus and her sick grandmother.

"It's a bad sign, isn't it?" I ask her when I've finished my story. "It's got to be a bad sign that, after two months of a pretty intense relationship, he doesn't want me to meet his parents and won't even talk about them with me."

"I don't know," Katrina says slowly, sipping on her lemonade. "Some guys move slow."

"I know. But usually slowness in dating meets getting together only once a week or taking a while to have sex. We haven't been slow about that. We jumped right into sex, and we get together almost every single day. It feels serious. And it's been two months of that kind of seriousness without any sort of commitment or opening up on his part."

"Is he hiding something, do you think? I don't mean something horrible like a wife or a criminal record. But maybe there's something about his background he doesn't want you to know?"

"Why not? I'm not a judgmental person. I don't think."

"You're definitely not."

"So why would he be afraid to tell me something?" I groan. "Maybe he's a spy and Dr. Evan Jones is a secret identity."

Katrina laughs as I knew she would. "I'm sure there's a good explanation for it. Some guys just move slow."

"I guess. But in my experience, guys who move slow are those who aren't really sure about the relationship. Guys who are sure don't keep putting on the brakes. So maybe..." My throat hurts so much I have to swallow over a lump. "Maybe he's just really along for the ride, as Marcus says. And he doesn't want me enough to make it real."

"Does he act like he wants you?"

"Yes. Unless I've turned into a clueless person, he acts like he wants me."

"And you want him?"

"More than I've ever wanted anyone."

Katrina's eyes are a combination of sympathetic and resigned. "Then you need to talk to him. Tell him the truth. The uncertainty is getting in the way of your happiness, so you need to deal with it." When I start to respond, she talks over me. "I know it's a risk. I know it could mean what you have is over. But if it's over from you wanting something so natural and reasonable, then it was never really yours to begin with."

My eyes burn, and my throat hurts, but I nod in response.

Because she's right.

I know she's right.

And I can no longer stall by saying it's too soon.

It's not too soon. It's time.

And if this relationship isn't going to be real, then it isn't a relationship at all.

I'VE RESOLVED to talk to Evan on Sunday evening. I know I need to do it now, so I'm not going to hesitate any longer. I figure we can get together for dinner, and I can bring it up easily by asking about how his time with his parents and Sara went.

But Evan texts in the afternoon to tell me that his family is staying in town for another night, so he won't be able to get together with me on Sunday after all.

It's like a blow to the gut.

It's not personal. I know it's not personal. Evan isn't wrong to prioritize time with his parents since he doesn't see them very often.

But I was all ready to have this discussion, and now I'm going to have to wait.

He's not in the office when I arrive on Monday morning, so I assume he's having breakfast with Sara and his parents before they leave town.

That's fine too. He has every reason to do so.

But the sight of his empty desk upsets me unduly.

I've got class at eight o'clock. And nine o'clock. And ten o'clock. And one o'clock. It's going to be the middle of the afternoon before I have the chance to really talk to him.

I teach my first three classes—not my most articulate of days—and I'm heading down the hall to our office suite when I run into Evan.

He's leaving the office, but he doesn't have his bag, so I assume he's just heading for the bathroom.

"Hey," I say with a smile. It feels like it's been forever since I've seen him. "I missed you this morning." I talk in my normal voice. It never occurs to me to do anything else.

"Yeah," he murmurs. "Had breakfast with Sara and my folks."

"How did that go? Did you have a good time with them?"

"It was fine." He's talking a lot softer than me and glancing up and down the hall.

I suddenly realize why. He doesn't want anyone to overhear us.

He doesn't want anyone to know we're having this conversation.

He's afraid someone is going to figure out there's something going on between us.

It hurts like a stab to the chest. There's no way I can hide my reaction. My eyes burn, and my lips wobble, and my voice breaks as I say, "I'm sorry. I didn't mean to let the world know that we actually talk to each other."

He obviously hears the hurt and bitterness in my voice because his face twists in surprise. "Beck?"

"Forget it," I rasp, turning back in the direction of the office. "Just forget it."

Wherever Evan had been planning to go, he doesn't do it now. As I hurry back to the office with my head ducked, he follows me.

He closes and locks the door behind us.

I'm standing in front of my desk, trying to control a surge of stupid tears.

"What the hell, baby?" he demands, coming up at my back. He'd probably have come around to face me, but my desk is in the way.

I take another minute to control myself, and then I turn around. "How do you think it makes me feel that you're embarrassed by me?"

His dark eyes widen in obvious surprise. "Embarrassed? Why the fuck would I be embarrassed?"

"I don't know! Maybe I'm not sophisticated enough or polished enough or thin enough or—"

"What the hell are you talking about?" he breaks in, gritting the words out between clenched teeth. He's angry.

I can see it in the flash of his eyes and the flush of his cheeks. "How dare you think that of me? You know very well that I think you're gorgeous and amazing. I've shown you that over and over again."

"You show it to me when we're in bed. And yes, I know you like to fuck me. You think that's the only thing that matters to me? What about the rest of our lives?"

"Where is this even coming from? We do a lot more than just have sex."

"I know we do, but we do it when no one else is around. So what am I supposed to think? You don't want anyone to know about us. You don't want me to know anything about your family. You only want to fuck me and hang out with me when it doesn't inconvenience anything else in your life."

I can see my words getting through to him. His expression twists again but with something other than anger this time. "I thought you've been happy with me," he rasps.

"I have been, but it's been more than two months now and nothing has changed. It's not enough. It's not enough."

"Why didn't you say something?"

I'm almost choking on my outrage. He's trying to blame this on me. "Because I didn't want to pressure you too soon and mess up a good thing. I'm trying not to be unreasonable. But I don't think it's unreasonable for me to want more than we have. I don't just want a sex partner. I want... I want something real."

I'm as naked and as vulnerable as I've ever been. Far

more so than when he's fucked my body. My heart is utterly exposed to him right now, and I have no idea how he'll respond.

He makes a sound in his throat and jerks his head to the side. He rubs at his jaw forcefully. "I'm sorry. I didn't know. I... I guess you can meet my parents if it's that important to you."

It's like a slap in the face. That's exactly how it feels. Because the words make me feel like I'm expecting something unreasonable when I know—I know—I'm not.

I jerk back in response to the pain and spit out, "Thank you so much for the reluctant gesture. You think that's what I want? You to do something you don't want to do just because you feel pressured into it by me. Why the hell do you think I didn't say anything earlier? This isn't what I want, Evan. I don't want to feel like a silly girl with ridiculous fantasies while you're like Aragorn stepping down off your pedestal to condescend to me. If it feels like you're taking a step down, then I don't want you at all."

This always happens to me. When I get going, I can't stop. Everything I feel comes pouring out, whether I want it to or not.

He's staring at me like I've transformed in front of his eyes.

But the words keep coming. "Because I'm not a silly girl. And I'm not some bloodless elf goddess who only appears to grace your life when all your important work is done. I'm a real human being with needs and fears and insecurities, but I'm also pretty damn special. I'm full of heart and passion and strength and devotion, and I'm ready to give all that to someone who really wants it. It's fine if you don't want it. But you better stop acting like you do. Because I'm not going to give everything to someone who only sees a small part of who I am and who won't give me everything too. Because that man doesn't deserve me."

"Beck," he says, reaching out to touch me. He sounds like he's soothing a wild animal.

"No! Don't try to settle me down. I don't want to be settled. I'm telling you, Dr. Evan Jones, I could kill the fucking Witch-king of Angmar if I had to, and the only man I want is the one who sees that. Who knows that. Who *wants* that."

His face has whitened, and there's something unspeakable in his eyes. His voice is hoarse when he says, "I do see that, Beck. I do want that."

My heart leaps in my chest. "Then prove it!"

He reaches out for me, and I know he's going to pull me into a kiss. I jerk away with a little sob. "I don't want to be kissed."

"Then what do you want?" He sounds almost as desperate as I feel.

The intensity of my emotion has climaxed, and it's leaving me with nothing but tears. They're starting to slide down my cheeks. I swipe one away. "If you don't know, then that's my answer."

I start to leave the office.

"Beck, wait. Don't just walk away."

I turn back to my desk and grab the books and notebook I need for my one-o'clock class and then grab my bag and hook it over my shoulder so I won't have to come back to the office afterward if I don't feel like it. "I'm not just walking away. I'm making a decision. I'm doing what's right for me. And I'm not going to settle for less than I deserve."

I leave then, before he can say something else and talk me out of what I know I have to do.

I manage to hold back the sobs as I hurry through the suite and down the hall toward the stairs.

I've got to make it to Jennifer's office. Hopefully, she's in there and available for a shoulder to cry on.

Because right now that's what I need.

8

Jennifer is in her office, and she helps me get myself together enough to teach my one o'clock.

It's not my finest teaching hour, but I manage to make it through.

When class is over, I go home. I don't have office hours or a meeting this afternoon, so there's no reason to stay on campus to be tortured by Evan's presence.

I need at least a day to recover before I see him again.

It's over with him. I know it is. For sure. Even if he had a few thoughts about us staying together for the long haul, I'm sure our conversations killed them dead. He probably thinks I'm being overdramatic and unreasonable. Maybe I am. I don't know.

All I know is that I can't keep holding on to a relationship that's not giving me what I need.

It feels horrible now. It feels like I've cut my heart out from my chest.

But it won't always feel this way. It will get better.

I can only pray it will get better soon.

I get in the shower when I get home and sob for a long time under the hot spray. Then I'm exhausted, so I change into lounge pants and a loose T-shirt and curl up on my couch under a throw blanket.

I turn on the TV and try to think of something to watch.

I need something familiar and comforting but that will absorb me emotionally enough to tune out my heartbreak for a while.

I'd usually watch The Lord of the Rings, but there's no way I can do that right now. The movies feel too close to Evan.

I turn on the first *Avengers* movie instead.

It doesn't distract me as much as I hoped, but I do feel better after it's done. I stay on the couch and wonder if I should make the effort to go out and get some ice cream. I don't have any in my freezer at the moment.

It's a serious failure of planning for emotional distress.

I haven't yet made a decision when there's a knock on my door.

I glance at the clock. Ten minutes after five.

I know who it is.

For just a minute I debate about whether I'm going to open the door for him. I know it's an unworthy feeling, but

I'm emotionally exhausted and I don't know how much more turmoil I can handle today.

But he keeps knocking, so I finally heft myself up off the couch and limp to the door. My hair is a mess. I'm not wearing a bra. My shoes and bag are still tossed on the floor of the entryway where I left them earlier.

I just don't care at the moment.

I open the door.

It's Evan, as I knew it would be.

I don't have the energy to smile at him or say anything. I just cling to the door and look at him.

He's in his suit with his jaw shaven and his hair trimmed short. His mouth is tight, and his eyes are strangely deep and aching.

Neither of us says anything for a long moment.

Then, "Can I please come in?" he asks gently. He's got a grocery bag in his hand, but I can't see what's in it.

I nod before I can make a conscious decision, and then I'm stuck stepping out of the way for him to walk in.

Then he's there. In my living room. Standing only a few feet away from me.

I twine my hands together behind my back and shift from foot to foot.

He clears his throat. Looks down at the floor. Then darts a quick glance up at my face. He looks almost vulnerable, and I don't know what to do with it. It makes my heart clench.

"You came over here," I say at last. "You have to talk first."

"Yeah." He lets out a long breath and moves his bag from one hand to the other. "I know."

Being me, I'm distracted by the most inconsequential thing. "What's in the bag?"

He extends his arms and opens the bag for me to see.

Two pints of gourmet ice cream.

"I, uh, would have been over here a few minutes sooner, but I had to stop by my house to pick them up first."

I burst into tears. Messy, helpless tears. It's so annoying, but there's no way I can help it.

"Oh damn, baby, please don't." He puts the bag on my console table and steps forward to pull me into his arms.

I try to respond, but I can't do anything but sob. I cry into his chest—making a complete mess on his nice suit coat—and I can't help but feel comforted by his strong, warm arms around me.

It can't be right. To let him comfort me when he's the one who made me cry.

It's not supposed to work this way.

It's a few minutes before my sobs lessen into little hiccups. Then I'm afraid to pull away from him. I don't want him to drop his arms. I don't want to have another painful conversation.

I just want things to continue the way they feel right

now. Like he cares about me. Like he wants to take care of me.

"Beck, baby, I'm so sorry about everything," he murmurs against my ear. "I had no idea you were upset about things, but that's not an excuse. I have been holding back on you, and I've known it all along. I shouldn't have done it, and I'm so sorry about it."

I can hardly believe what I'm hearing. I have to straighten up and pull away so I can see his face and affirm it's really him and that he means it.

He does. His eyes hold mine, and they're as sober as I've ever seen them.

And, let me tell you, that's pretty damn sober.

I sniff and wipe at my face. "You didn't have to open up to me if you didn't want to. If you weren't serious. Just because I want you to be, doesn't mean you have to—"

"You don't get it," he breaks in. "I was serious. I am serious. I've been serious about you from the very beginning. There's no one else in the world I've ever felt this way about. I wanted you from the moment I saw you, and every day I've known you makes me want you more. I wasn't holding back because I didn't want to be close to you. I did. I do. So much."

I can't believe this is happening. I hug my arms to my chest. "So why were you holding back?"

"Because I was afraid that if you saw me for real, you wouldn't want me after all."

My throat closes up around my words. I have to try

three times to get them out. "But... but... but... why wouldn't I want you?"

"Because I'm not a very good catch. I don't have much experience with women, and I don't know what I'm doing most of the time. I'm not cool or confident or particularly interesting. I can talk about books and ideas but not much else. And... I've spent my life feeling not good enough."

"Why would you ever think that? You're so brilliant, and you're so hot."

His mouth twists in a dry little smile. "I think you're the only person who's really thought I was hot."

"That's not true! You are. Other women definitely see it too. Evan, I don't understand how you could think I wouldn't—"

"It's not you. It's me. It's me. My parents..." He glances away with a tightening of his features, like he's forcing himself to continue. "It wasn't that I was embarrassed to introduce you to my parents. It was that I was embarrassed to introduce them to you. They're..." He shakes his head. "They're assholes, Beck. There's no other way to describe it. They're narrow-minded and ignorant and racist, and they've never really liked me. They wanted two sons like my brother, and they only got one. I wasn't anything like him. They were always disappointed in me. My brother grew up and worked for my dad at his car dealership, and I became one of those elite academics who're trying to force their ridiculous ideas on the rest of the world. That's actually what they think. When they came to visit this weekend, I would have loved for you to meet Sara, but you'd have had to meet my parents too. And I knew if you were there that they'd be terrible. They always are. They'd put me down, and they'd probably put you down, and you'd see it and hate them and want to get as far away as possible. You're way too good for them. You're way too good for me."

"I am not too good for you!" I burst out, overwhelmed by this revelation. "I don't care about your parents, except that they've obviously hurt you a lot. So they're assholes. A lot of people have shitty parents. It doesn't change who you are. And you're not like that. You're not. I'm not too good for you."

My impassioned outburst has an effect. His face twists with emotion, and he reaches out to cup my face. "But you are, baby. Because you've been in this all the way from the very beginning, and I've been holding back because I'm so scared of losing you."

"I've been scared too," I whisper, reaching for the lapels of his jacket. One of them is still damp from my tears. "I've wanted to say something for a long time, but I didn't want to trap you in a conversation you didn't want and scare you away. So maybe both of us messed up a little."

"You could never mess up. You're never anything but amazing. Beautiful and brilliant and passionate and sweet and generous and sexy as hell."

I giggle stupidly. "And kind of flighty."

"I like that about you."

I giggle again, pulling myself closer to him. "And still a little insecure."

"So am I. So is everyone. I love every single thing about you, Beck, even the things you believe are faults."

I gasp and stare up at him in astonished delight. "You do?"

"Yes. Of course I do. How could I not?"

"Then... Then you understand how I feel about you. I don't care about all the things you're worried about. I love every single thing about you too."

His eyes transform with a joy and relief so palpable it traps my breath. "Really?"

"Really."

"And you don't mind that my parents are terrible human beings who've always treated me like I'm worthless?"

"No. I don't care about that, except to be angry you've had to deal with it." I suddenly realize something. I gasp and cover my mouth with one hand.

"What?" he asks, a confused frown taking over the soft, fond joy on his face.

"You really are Faramir, aren't you?"

He freezes for a moment as he processes the question. Then he bursts into laughter and pulls me into a tight hug. "I guess I am. Complete with a dad who prefers my older brother to me. But at least I can recognize the most incredible woman in the world when I see her and want nothing else but her, so maybe Faramir's not a bad man to be."

I squeeze him as tightly as I can. Then I pull his face down toward me and say just before I kiss him, "I wouldn't want you to be anyone else."

EVENTUALLY WE COLLAPSE on my couch, cover up with the throw blanket, and eat both pints of ice cream.

Evan has taken off his jacket, tie, shirt, and shoes, and he's wearing just his trousers, undershirt, and socks. He might not be quite as comfortable as I am—in just my lounge pants and T-shirt with no bra—but he doesn't seem to mind.

We end up stretched out on the couch together, still too emotional to have sex.

I am at least. And he doesn't seem to be in a hurry to pull out of our full-body hug.

We've been lying in silence for a long time, just relaxing together, and I think he might have actually fallen asleep, so I raise my head to check.

His eyes are open. Soft and nakedly fond and completely vulnerable.

I gulp. "Hi."

He chuckles and strokes my hair back from my face. "Hi."

"Just checking to see if you're asleep."

"I'm not asleep. I'm not sure how it's possible to sleep when you're as happy as I am now."

"Really?"

"Yes, really. Did you not understand what I was saying before?"

"I understand. It's just hard for me to process that all my dreams seem to be coming true."

"They're my dreams too," he says, rubbing his cheek against mine. "I've spent my life dreaming of someone who would see me for real, want who I am, and love me completely."

I sniff like the sap I am. "I do. And I've spent my whole life dreaming of the same thing."

We hug again for a minute and then settle back in a more comfortable position. He's on his back, and I'm fit against his side, half on top of him with my cheek resting on his shoulder.

I ask him, "So you really were interested in me from the very beginning?"

"Of course I was. How could I not be? I was all focused on doing a good job in my new position and getting my book done and trying to spend some time with my sister when you just sort of exploded into my life—all hair and cleavage and lips and laughter and passion and sweetness. I don't think I made it through the first ten minutes of meeting you before I started imagining taking you to bed. Then the more I got to know you, the more I wanted you. Not just in my bed but in my life. I couldn't believe when you kissed me. It never even occurred to me that you'd want me too. Then when we started having sex, it was so good I was afraid of messing it up. So I tried to play it cool and act like it was a normal beginning to a relationship instead of one lovesick fool always drooling over you."

I snicker at that, although my heart is a puddle of good in my chest. "You did a good job of acting cool. I had no idea."

"I've learned how to not let my feelings show. That was a weakness I couldn't risk in my family."

My swoony smile fades into a frown. "It's not right that you were made to feel that way. You never have to hide things or act cool with me."

He starts pressing kisses against my mouth. My right cheek. My throat. "That's good to know."

His kisses continue, and soon I'm responding with all the passion in my heart. He takes off my clothes and kisses and caresses me all over until I'm babbling out my pleasure and need and grinding against him uninhibitedly.

He seems to like me in this state. He keeps teasing me until I'm begging for him to make me come. When he finally does—with his hands and his mouth—I can't hold back my loud cries of release. They echo through the house.

Maybe outside the house. I don't know and I don't care.

Nothing has ever felt as good as being with Evan like this. Having him love me like this.

When he's finally gotten his fill of pleasing me, he takes off the rest of his clothes. Since I've already come a few times, I can take my time in making him feel good too.

I kiss and touch him all over. I wrap my lips around his erection and suck a few times, making him groan in the most erotic way.

Then I let him slip out of my mouth, and he turns me over on my hands and knees with my butt up in the air. He takes me from behind. I look at him over my shoulder, and he leans over to kiss me as he pushes his way in.

We've forgotten the condom. I realize it after he's fully inside me.

"Shit," he mutters, freezing in place. "The condom."

"It's fine," I tell him. "I'm on birth control. I want you just like this."

He doesn't argue. Just closes his eyes and moans as he makes his first slow thrust.

The slow rhythm doesn't last for long. Soon he's eager and forceful, pumping his hips fast and bumping his pelvis against my bottom to make a sexy, slapping sound.

I'm so far gone from foreplay and the revelation of love that I'm coming before I'm prepared for it. I sob loud and sloppy as a climax overtakes me. I shake with the sensations until my whole body is jiggling wildly.

"Oh fuck, baby," he gasps, pushing against my contractions. "I love you so much. There's never been anyone in the world like you."

I come again from his words. Or maybe I never stopped coming.

He's coming too, so both of us are shaking and jerking.

The couch is rocking wildly as we work through the spasms of release.

We collapse together in a tangle of hot flesh, limp limbs, and loud gasping. He rearranges me so he can hold me close. I'm sore and wet between my legs from his fluids and mine. It's almost uncomfortable.

I don't care. I don't want to be anywhere but here.

"I love you," I whisper, kissing his shoulder.

"I love you too. I can't believe you're really mine."

I smile. "Well, I am. And as long as you're mine, I'll be yours too."

A MONTH LATER, I'm grading papers in the office and grumbling every time I get to the bottom of a page.

Grumbling in my mind. Most of the time, I manage to keep myself from doing it out loud.

While it would be nice to believe that finding love could make my problems go away, grading papers is a struggle that even the greatest of love can't assuage.

They're painful. And these are the most painful papers to grade of the semester because they're sophomore-level research papers.

My upper-level papers are longer, but they also tend to be better.

Most of these are just terrible, and a couple are clearly downloaded from online without even the slightest attempt to mask the cheating.

I'm scowling at a particularly boring paper—it's not plagiarized, but it's also as tedious as a paper can get—when Evan returns from his second class of the day.

It's Tuesday, so he's got two classes in the morning and one long one at six in the evening.

He laughs as he puts his stuff down on his desk.

"What's so funny?" I ask, slanting him a peeved look since no one should be laughing while I'm tortured by papers to grade.

"Your face. Surely they're not that bad." His eyes are warm and affectionate, although his mouth is just barely twitching with a smile.

"They're terrible!" I moan, dropping my head onto my desk in an exaggerated gesture of despair. "How can anyone write so bad?"

He laughs again and comes over to read my computer screen over my shoulder. "Well," he says, after reading for a minute. "I think this person is in my British lit class. How many people can use an apostrophe wrong in so many unique and disastrous ways?"

I giggle and grab his hand, pulling it to my face to plant a kiss on his palm. I drop it quickly though since I want to finish this paper before lunch.

He leaves me alone to do so as he puts his stuff away and checks his email. He's quiet for so long I look over as I'm writing my final comments on the paper. He's loosened his tie (just slightly), and he's leaning back in his desk chair as far as it will go.

He's giving me the sweetest little smile.

I have to fight not to smile back. "Are you sitting there watching me suffer?"

"You do it so dramatically. It's fascinating to watch."

"If I recall, this weekend you were muttering out historic curses while you were grading your Renaissance lit papers, so I don't think you have any grounds to judge me."

"I'm not judging you, baby. I'm enjoying you. It's not even close to the same thing."

I shake my head at him, trying to maintain a disapproving expression. Failing utterly. "Well, try to enjoy me in quiet. I've got to think of something insightful to say about this paper."

"Just write this: *I can tell you've done some thinking on this topic, and you've found a few good sources. But you need to strengthen your argument and use your research more effectively. And your writing needs a lot more proofreading.*"

I gape at him in astonishment. "How could you possibly get all that from just scanning a couple of paragraphs over my shoulder?"

"Did I get it right? I swear I end up writing that exact thing on about half my papers."

I give him an eye roll as I turn back to my computer. So sue me. I write one of his sentences down in my comments verbatim and then shrug and add the proofreading sentence too.

Then I slap a C- on the paper and close out the document, uploading it to the online class portal before I close that out too.

"Halfway done," I announce. I glance at the clock and see that it's almost noon. "You ready to go down to lunch?"

"I'm ready." He stands up and buttons his suit.

The gesture is so Evan-like that I go over and give him a quick hug.

He returns the hug, looking both surprised and pleased. Then we head downstairs and outside to find that Marcus and Jennifer are standing next to the fountain in the middle of campus, waiting for us.

Marcus has his arm around Jennifer, and he's grinning as we approach.

He looks happy. Both of them do. They're getting married in a couple of months.

I'm not even thinking about marriage yet—other than a few random flickers of possibility that pass quickly through my mind and don't bother me. It's not time for Evan and me yet. We haven't been together for very long, and we both have had a lot to work through to come together the way we have.

I haven't met his parents yet, but I've joined him a few times for lunch with his sister on Saturdays.

I never have doubts about Evan's feelings anymore. We're going to get there eventually.

I'm not in any hurry. I'm going to enjoy the stage we're in right now.

He takes my hand as we approach Jennifer and Marcus and keeps holding it as we greet them. We have a brief conversation about where we're going to lunch, and we decide to walk to a sandwich place that's just four blocks away from campus.

Evan gives me a little kiss as we start walking. We're right in the middle of campus, and there's a lot of people around to see.

I'm getting used to it. It doesn't bother me that much that he and I are a hot source of gossip.

Pretty soon no one will care that I fell in love with my office mate. And maybe a little part of me likes that I'm the girl the most eligible man around fell for.

I've never been that girl before.

He's a lot more than that to me though. He sees me for who I am and loves me for it, exactly as I do him.

There are no guarantees in this life, but I don't think that's going to change.

I was waiting for my Faramir, but what I've found is even better.

EPILOGUE

Six months later, I'm in the library checking to make sure there are enough books available for my students to use for their research topics this semester. I should be able to check the catalog, but I learned a long time ago to also check the shelves to ensure the books are there and easily identifiable, or I'll have students whining that they couldn't find anything to use.

I have to make them use at least two books and two articles from academic journals, or they'll end up with nothing but the most shallow of internet sources.

Once I've verified that there's enough available for them to be without an excuse, I start down the back stairwell to the ground floor. I've run out of excuses now. I've done every piddly thing on my to-do list and emptied out my email inbox.

I'll have to start grading papers now.

No more artificial delays.

When I reach the bottom of the stairs and open the door, I stop in surprise. The facilities crew is here moving furniture around.

I wave at a couple of guys I know, but they look busy so I don't stop to ask them what's going on. Instead, I see Katrina behind the research help desk, and I head over toward her.

"What are they doing?" I ask when I reach her.

"We're redoing this whole section to make an exhibit space for art."

"Oh really? That's a nice idea."

"I know." She rolls her violet-blue eyes.

"Why do you look so annoyed? Don't you like the idea?"

"I do like the idea. It's a great place for art students to have their stuff displayed. But I suggested something similar a year and a half ago, and Martha completely refused to hear it." Martha is her boss, the director of the library.

"So what changed her mind now?"

Katrina's lashes narrow into a familiar look of dry skepticism that's characteristic of her. "The new guy who's been teaching art classes in the evening."

"I heard they had a new adjunct, and people seem to really like him. You don't like him?"

Her expression clears. "I don't know him. I'm sure he's fine. Students definitely seem to like him. But he's one of those guys who clearly always gets his way because he's so hot."

"He's hot?"

"He's definitely hot. But he seems to have that way about him that can talk people into anything without even trying. Martha wouldn't even hear a word from me about it, but all he had to do was mention it, and look what happens." She waves toward the activity in the far wing of the main floor. "I'm sorry. I shouldn't be so pissy about it. It just annoys me. My ex-boyfriend was the same way. He could talk me into anything, and I was so spineless I went along."

I've been smiling, since her annoyance is kind of amusing, but the last comment sobers me up. "I'm sure you weren't spineless."

She shakes her head. "I had less spine than I should've. I don't know why. I've always kind of been that way with men. I just let them lead me around. I've been trying date some, but I realized I was starting to do the same thing. Focus only on them and not on what I want for myself."

"So what are you going to do?"

"I'm calling a moratorium on dating until I get my life the way I want it. I don't need a guy to get what I want out of life, and I'm tired of waiting around for it." She gives me an observant look. "You didn't wait around. You got a PhD. You got a good job. You got a house and a lot of friends, and then when you met Evan, he just sort of fit into the life you already established for yourself. That's what I want too."

I reach out to squeeze her upper arm encouragingly. "I'm sure you can do it. You've got a good start. You started that second graduate program, and you've been working on the other things. I think it's a good idea to not worry about guys for a while. If it happens, it happens. It's not the only important thing in life."

She nods determinedly and smiles at me. "That's exactly right. That's going to be my attitude from now on. You're a good example for me."

"I'm not sure I should be anyone's example, but focusing on yourself sounds like an excellent plan. And just let me know if you need anyone to remind you to keep on track."

"I'm sure I will."

Glancing at my watch, I make a face. "Okay. Back to my office. I've got papers to grade."

"Say hi to Evan for me."

I smile at the sound of Evan's name and give Katrina a wave as I leave the library.

I've never really thought of myself as a good example for anyone else, but maybe I can be. Maybe I am. I've made plenty of mistakes just like everyone else, but I'm really happy with my life. With what I've accomplished. With my friends and family.

With Evan.

We're still sharing an office, but he'll be getting his own

in the fall since Professor Cole is finally going to retire and vacate his office. In a way, it makes me sad since I like the time I spend with Evan in our office. But it makes sense for us to have our own space at work, and if he refuses Cole's office, it might be a long time before another good one comes available for him.

He'll still be on the same floor as me—just one suite away—so it's not like I'll never get to see him at work.

And maybe soon we'll be living together.

We spend most nights together as it is, so I think it's likely he'll want us to move in together soon.

I hope so.

I want everything with Evan, and every month that passes makes me want it even more.

Shaking the thought away, I reach the main academic building and force myself to walk up the stairs instead of taking the elevator. I always get less exercise at the end of the semesters when my workload picks up, and walking the stairs is the least I can do.

I'm out of breath and dreading the papers waiting for me when I reach the office. Evan is at his computer, working on the final chapter of his book.

"Hey," I say breathlessly.

He mumbles out a response, his eyes never leaving his computer screen. I don't mind. He's trying to get his book done by the deadline as well as teaching his four classes this semester. It's not easy. He's been working really hard, and I'm not going to distract him right now.

Pretty soon the spring semester will be over and we'll both have the summer free of classes. We can have some fun then.

I collapse into my desk chair and grin at the side of his head.

He doesn't see me. His tie is just slightly loosened. He's almost due for a haircut, and one tuft of hair is sticking out askew. His expression is adorably serious.

I love him so much.

He shifts in his chair and clears his throat. It's an oddly fidgety gesture that isn't at all like him. I frown as I study him, and so I see when he slants a quick look over at me.

I thought he was totally focused on his writing, but he's not.

"What's the matter?" I ask.

He frowns and doesn't look at me. "Nothing."

"Don't give me that. You think I don't know you? Tell me what's wrong."

"Nothing's wrong. I thought you were going to grade papers this afternoon." He sounds almost bad-tempered. That's not like him either.

"I am. But I don't want to."

"Well, they're not going to go away just because you want them to."

Now I'm frowning too. "What's gotten into you?" With a huff, I turn my chair so it's facing my computer.

I was in a good mood, but Evan is being weird, and I really don't want to grade papers.

I've poised my fingers over the keyboard when I finally realize that something has been placed there.

On my keyboard.

Something that doesn't belong.

It's a small jeweler's box. The top is open.

Inside is a pretty diamond ring. An emerald cut solitaire on an engraved platinum band.

I gape down at it like a fool.

It takes a long time to process what I'm seeing. Then it takes a long time for me to turn my head toward Evan.

He's looking at me now with a tiny smile on his lips.

As I stare speechlessly, his smile fades.

"If it's too soon, I'll take it back," he says, slowly rising to his feet. "Or if you don't want it at all."

"I do!" I burst out. I'm fumbling as I reach for the ring. "Don't you dare take it back."

His face transforms with relief as he walks over to close and lock the office door. Then he comes over beside my chair. He reaches over to take the ring from the box I'm holding. Then he kneels onto one knee.

"I love you, Beck. More than anything. I never dreamed I'd find anyone like you to love and be loved by, but I'm not going to let you go now that I have. So I'll be your Faramir forever, if you'll be my Éowyn. Marry me. Please?"

It all hits me in a rush, and I burst into tears.

His mouth parts slightly as he stares.

I try to pull it together so I can get a coherent word out, but I'm so overwhelmed that it takes me a minute.

He doesn't want to wait a minute. He adjusts on his knee uncomfortably. "Baby, I don't know what this means."

I sob again and fling myself at him. "It means yes!"

My flinging was a bit too hard. We both tumble to the floor.

He doesn't seem to mind. He's laughing as he eases me off him, turning us both on our sides so we're facing each other. He cups my cheek and kisses me, right there on the floor.

I kiss him back with a wave of passion that cannot be held back.

"If you'll hold on a minute," he mumbles against my lips, "I can put on the ring."

"Okay." I make myself pull away, grinning and sniffing as he slides the ring onto my finger.

Then I kiss him again.

And this time I don't stop.

ABOUT NOELLE ADAMS

Noelle handwrote her first romance novel in a spiral-bound notebook when she was twelve, and she hasn't stopped writing since. She has lived in eight different states and currently resides in Virginia, where she writes full time, reads any book she can get her hands on, and offers tribute to a very spoiled cocker spaniel.

She loves travel, art, history, and ice cream. After spending far too many years of her life in graduate school, she has decided to reorient her priorities and focus on writing contemporary romances. For more information, please check out her website: noelle-adams.com.

Made in the USA
Monee, IL
12 October 2023